D0290211

THE
WAITING
SKY

BY THE AUTHOR OF

The Implosion of Aggie Winchester

Donut Days

THE
WAITING
SKY

LARA ZIELIN

G. P. PUTNAM'S SONS

AN IMPRINT OF PENGUIN GROUP (USA) INC.

G. P. PUTNAM'S SONS • A division of Penguin Young Readers Group.
Published by The Penguin Group.
Penguin Group (USA) Inc., 375 Hudson Street, New York, NY 10014, U.S.A.
Penguin Group (Canada), 90 Eglinton Avenue East, Suite 700, Toronto, Ontario M4P 2Y3, Canada
(a division of Pearson Penguin Canada Inc.).
Penguin Books Ltd, 80 Strand, London WC2R 0RL, England.
Penguin Ireland, 25 St. Stephen's Green, Dublin 2, Ireland (a division of Penguin Books Ltd.).
Penguin Group (Australia), 250 Camberwell Road, Camberwell, Victoria 3124, Australia
(a division of Pearson Australia Group Pty Ltd).
Penguin Books India Pvt Ltd, 11 Community Centre, Panchsheel Park, New Delhi—110 017, India.
Penguin Group (NZ), 67 Apollo Drive, Rosedale, Auckland 0632, New Zealand
(a division of Pearson New Zealand Ltd).
Penguin Books (South Africa) (Pty) Ltd, 24 Sturdee Avenue, Rosebank,
Johannesburg 2196, South Africa.
Penguin Books Ltd, Registered Offices: 80 Strand, London WC2R 0RL, England.

Design by Marikka Tamura.
Text set in Maxime Std.
Library of Congress Cataloging-in-Publication Data
Zielin, Lara, 1975–
The waiting sky / Lara Zielin.   p. cm.
Summary: Minnesota seventeen-year-old Jane McAllister has devoted years to helping her
out-of-control, alcoholic mother, but joining her brother in chasing tornadoes for a summer gives
her a fresh perspective, new options, and her first real romance.
[1. Storm chasers—Fiction. 2. Tornadoes—Fiction. 3. Brothers and sisters—Fiction. 4. Mothers and
daughters—Fiction. 5. Alcoholism—Fiction. 6. Family problems—Fiction.] I. Title.
PZ7.Z497Vor 2012   [Fic]—dc23   2011025539
ISBN 978-0-399-25686-8
1 3 5 7 9 10 8 6 4 2

For Deb

"When you used to tell me that you chase tornadoes, deep down I thought it was just a metaphor."

—*Twister*

"Whenever people talk to me about the weather, I always feel quite certain that they mean something else. And that makes me so nervous."

—*The Importance of Being Earnest*

1

Even though there's a black wedge of sky in front of me that might drop a twister at any second, I can't get my mom's voice out of my head. Not even the sirens blasting in the nearby town can drown it out.

"Come back home."

"I miss you so much."

"I'm no good without my Janey."

It's Jane, not Janey, I tell her in my mind. Plain Jane. Rain-wrapped Jane. Never-again Jane.

Not that I ever say anything. In real life, I let her call me whatever she wants because, let's face it, reasoning with a drunk is a lot like trying to train a chicken. After a while, you just let the thing squawk and flap and hope it doesn't escape the coop.

The sky is really rotating now. The Tornado Brothers—or Torbros for short—have all gone quiet, waiting. The sirens are lost in the howling wind.

At the far corner of the field we're standing in, a tornado starts to descend. Dust on the ground whips up. I see the manic swirls of dirt and hay and grass, and there's my mom again—all chaos and mess . . . and cleanup when it's over.

"Jane! You getting pictures?" My brother, Ethan, is smiling, pointing at the clouds. The winds have whisked his reddish-blond hair into a fauxhawk, which would be hilarious if he wasn't standing a quarter mile away from a spinning vortex of death. But in the mouth of Mother Nature's fury, Ethan's totally at ease, and I wonder if it's because he's studied weather for years, or because he figured out a long time ago that the things that really hurt you don't usually fall from the sky.

I hoist the camera hanging around my neck and start snapping photos, even though I'm still not used to taking pictures in all this wind. The pressure changes are making my ears pop, and my mouth is clamped tight since I got dirt stuck in my teeth last week. But still, dirty teeth and life-threatening storms are better than being back in Minnesota, with my mom stumbling in and out of the apartment, and my best friend, Cat, trying to make my life Leave-It-to-Beaver perfect like hers, which I guess I shouldn't be mad about. At least she's trying to do something—trying in her way to help me—which is more than what I'd do if my best friend had almost killed me.

The storm is roaring, but the twister can't decide what it wants to do. Wispy funnels form again and again but don't stick around long enough to become full-fledged tornadoes. I snap a picture of Ethan, his head tilted back, staring at the sky. It's a funny moment to realize we have the same nose, but I guess we do—thin and straight and strong. It's physical proof we're related, I think. Biology's way of linking us on the outside since on the inside we're so different. Like how Ethan has a tendency to abandon people, and I'm the stick-around type. Or at least I was.

Eventually he tears his eyes away from the clouds to yell at Stephen, the six-foot-six founder of Torbros. "Storm's moving off!"

"Yeah, but 'nother one's coming!" Stephen hollers back, his voice rumbly like thunder. I look where he's pointing, and sure enough, after a short break in the clouds, there's another bruise-colored sky headed our way.

I know this is the part where I'm supposed to feel the rush, supposed to get all excited about Mother Nature's unpredictability, but the truth is I don't. I'm not a weather junkie. I'm just here to take pictures for the Torbros website, a summer job Ethan rigged for me. Normally, I never would have left Mom for a day, much less a whole summer. But Ethan asked, and things at home were pretty messed up after what happened with Cat. So here I am. End of story.

Except that it's not the end of the story. Not by a long shot—especially now that Ethan's asked me to live with him after the weather season's wrapped.

As if he knows I'm thinking about him, Ethan's face looms suddenly at the end of my lens. "We gotta go," he says over the wind. "Hail in a minute. Get to the van." He doesn't even wait for me to reply—he just runs off to help load up some of the equipment with our tech guy, Mason, who has freckles covering practically every square inch of his body.

I let the camera go and start jogging toward the van, but I stop when I reach Hallie, the one "sister" among the Tornado Brothers. She's kneeling in the prairie grass, hunched over Polly, one of our weather instruments. The muscles on her thin arms strain as she works to adjust knobs and levers.

"Hey," I say, raising my voice against the storm, "we gotta hustle! Hail any second."

Hallie looks up, and her normally pretty face is crumpled. Her brown eyes remind me of the splintered wood and crushed houses we see after a tornado. "The data's gone," she says. "I can't get Polly to work." The wind tosses her words so quickly that I almost don't catch them.

I glance at Polly's spinning instruments, taking in the buttons, switches, and meters covering her stainless-steel core the size of a small microwave. I don't understand everything about how Polly works, but I know that—one—the Torbros love her and say she's going to put them ahead of every other chaser in the field, and—two—we have to get her out of here because the minute that hail comes crashing down, Polly is toast.

"Where's Victor?" I ask. Victor is Stephen's brother and co-founder of the Torbros. He had shirts made that said TORBROS: WE CHASE CHICKS AND STORMS, and when Hallie and I said we didn't want to wear them, he told us we should change the word *chicks* to *dicks,* like that was all it took. Victor's also the brainchild behind Polly, so anything that happens with her, he takes personally.

4

"He went to get something from the van," Hallie says. "The minute he took off, Polly crashed. I wanted to get her up and running before he came back."

I squint at the vehicle, but I can't see Victor. He must be inside it, all buckled in, ready to take off. Which is nuts. If Victor has put his own safety over Polly's, then the weather is about to get seriously bad.

"Hallie," I say, pulling on her arm, "come on. Get up. Victor's not coming back. I'll help you carry Polly, but we need to move. Now."

Hallie shakes her head, fiddling some more with Polly's instrumentation. "No way. If I leave now, Victor will never let this go."

On our last chase, Victor made a point of saying that women belong in the lab, analyzing data—not out on chases. Me he tolerates because, technically, I'm not doing any of the scientific work. But Hallie—not so much. Which makes this whole situation more than a little ironic, considering Hallie's the one out here trying to jump-start his supposedly beloved project, all while he's sitting in the van.

"Hallie—" I want to tell her that if Victor tries to say anything about Polly crashing, she can point out his ass-in-the-van neglect. But she doesn't let me finish.

"Give me two minutes."

I look at the churning green sky and feel the ice-cold air through my long-sleeved shirt. Hallie knows as well as I do we don't have two minutes. The rest of the team is already in the van, save Ethan, who's standing next to it. He cups his hands around his mouth and yells something at us, but it's lost in the frigid, shrieking air.

"Hallie," I say, praying her name comes out like it does at home, when I say "Mom," after things have gone far enough.

The steely, determined look in Hallie's eyes ebbs. "I know," she says finally. "I know I'm being stupid. I just—God. Victor's going to be such an asshat about this."

I nod, thinking we're going to get back to the van just fine, when the first hailstone lands on my shoulder. "Ow!"

"Shit!" Hallie yells. She scrambles to her feet, and together we haul Polly out of the grass, racing as fast as we can toward the van.

Hail pelts my back and shoulders and head. I bend over Polly, trying to protect her, and Hallie does the same. I think about stories I've read where people get stoned to death and wonder if this is what they experienced. My body is on fire.

When we reach the van, my brother and Stephen are just inside the sliding door. Their hands are outstretched, their faces white. They pull Polly from us first, then I toss Hallie at them. One last stone comes crashing down on my head as I throw myself into the van. Everything goes fuzzy and gray.

My mom reaches me in my haze.

"You're there for Polly—for a machine—but you won't come back to me in Minnesota?"

I'm not sure if the pain I feel is from the hailstones or the guilt.

My brother's talking to me, but his voice is underwater. We're all floating on dark waves. I press my palms against my eyes and let the blackness suck at me. I picture a twister carrying me up and away—past the clouds and over the rainbow—back to Minnesota. "Where you belong," my mom says. "Home."

Except, of course, that Minnesota doesn't feel like home. Not anymore, anyway. Neither does Oklahoma. Or Nebraska. Or Kansas, for that matter.

I can click my heels together all I want, but there's just no place to go.

2

By ten o'clock that night, I'm sitting outside in a plastic pool chair at a Days Inn. We're still in Oklahoma. I think. Nothing about the flat-packed plains beyond the pool's edge or the long line of lights on the freeway says for sure, one way or another.

A breeze picks up and ripples the water. The pool is empty—it closed an hour ago—and I'm the only one around, which is a good thing. If legions of kids were still swimming, screaming, and splashing water at each other, the dull throb above my left temple would be even worse.

The hailstone knocked me out for only a second, but my brother still called off the chase and made me go to an urgent care clinic. While the remaining four Torbros sat in the parking lot, we saw a doctor who told me to call him if I got dizzy or nauseous or couldn't remember stuff. But ultimately he said I was fine; it was just a nasty bump on the head.

I glance up as Victor files by, just on the other side of the pool's metal gate. In the glare of the motel's lights, I can see he's carrying Polly. One of her dials is cracked, and I want to call out to him—to ask him if Polly's going to be okay—but I decide against it. If Polly *is* broken, he might try to blame Hallie for it. And then I might try to defend Hallie, which could lead to a fight, and getting into it with Victor might not be the smartest idea ever. Even in the low light, I can see the pale scar that runs from his temple to his jaw. It's the kind of scar that you get in a bar, where a piece of a broken beer bottle slices through your skin, or at least that's what I imagine. Best to get news about Polly from someone else later, I think.

My phone buzzes, interrupting my thoughts. I pull it out and stare at the text. Hope ur ok. I am thinking abt u.

I stare at Cat's message until the letters blur. I try to text back, but my hands shake so hard, I almost drop the phone.

Cat.

The accident.

I can still smell the dusty interior of our battered Honda that day, when my mom drove Cat and me home from the mall. I can still see the way the sunlight lit up Cat's cornflower-blue eyes when she talked about the cute guy in the food court. I can feel the silky fabric of the scarf I bought at the mall's resale boutique. A vintage piece for sure, probably 1920s was my guess, and a steal at five bucks.

And then.

And then the screech of tires on blacktop, the shrill sound of the horn, Cat and me getting pitched forward so hard, our seat belts locked.

We were in the middle of an intersection. My mom had run a red light.

"Mom!" I cried as a car with the right of way sped past our hood. Another horn blared. My mom tried to gun it, but cars were still speeding around us.

"What the hell?" my mom yelled.

Time slowed way down. A little squeak escaped Cat, who was staring out her window, watching a truck barrel straight toward her. All I could make out was a grill and glinting chrome.

In the space of a half second, a thousand thoughts ignited my frontal lobe. *My mom is drunk. We are stopped in the middle of an intersection. A truck is coming toward us. Mom's reaction times are slow. We'll be lucky if she hits the accelerator by the time the truck is on top of us.*

Finally, my adrenaline kicked in. "Go!" I screamed, hitting my mom's seat so hard her head snapped forward. "Drive now!"

Somehow, Mom's pickled brain responded. We jerked into motion as another car swerved around our front, its horn thundering. I thought I smelled burning rubber, and wondered if it was our tires, or the tires of the truck that was now so close, I thought I could see the wide eyes and open mouth of its driver.

We were moving, but the truck still clipped our rear, shattering the back windshield. Glass came raining down on Cat and me in razor-sharp drops. The Honda spun around again and again. I remember thinking there was an earthquake happening, and what a funny time for that to occur—in Minnesota, no less, where we weren't supposed to have them. It wasn't until later I realized the whole car was shaking with the tremor of the truck's ginormous wheels, inches from running us all over.

When the world stopped spinning and shaking, the car was on the other side of the intersection—facing the right way, of all things. As if nothing had happened.

Except, when I looked out the now-missing back windshield—where scraps of glass clung to the edges like those stalagmites we learned about in fourth-grade geology—I saw the truck that had rammed us was jackknifed in the middle of the intersection. Two more cars had come careering to a halt at odd angles around it.

I looked over at Cat, my mouth open. Blood was trickling down her face from her left eyebrow, where a piece of glass the size of a bottle cap was wedged in her skin. There was a sour taste in my throat, and I wondered if it was the taste of fear. "Cat—"

My voice faltered. There were no words for this. Cat's eyes, round and wide, found mine. Her mouth moved, but no sound came out. It wasn't until two drops of blood landed on the seat fabric that I realized I was hurt, too. I had no idea where, though. I couldn't feel anything.

My mom grunted, then shook her head like a prizefighter after taking a right hook to the temple. The next thing I knew, we were moving.

Cat gargled something. She whipped her head toward my mom, then back at the accident scene. The car was shuddering and vibrating, its jacked-up back end trying to keep pace with the front.

Cat grabbed my hand. "She c-can't leave," she stuttered. "It w-was an accid-d-d-ent." Cat's jaw trembled like she was freezing cold.

My mom couldn't hear her, or was pretending not to. The accident scene was getting farther and farther away.

We passed a few cars where all the drivers had their eyes trained on the truck in the middle of the intersection. They didn't even notice us. They had no idea we were the cause of the mess they were staring at—and were driving away.

As soon as she could, my mom swung onto back streets, weaving in and out of quiet neighborhoods to stay off the main roads. Cat gripped my left hand with both of hers. With my right hand, I took my vintage scarf and held it just below the cut in her eyebrow. Blood stained the fabric bright red.

"M-m-make her go back," Cat whispered. "This is *wr-wr-wrong.*"

My insides twisted. How could I tell her I understood what my mom was doing? "We don't have any insurance," I imagined myself saying. "We can't afford it. If any of those people sued us, we'd lose everything. Plus, if they gave my mom a Breathalyzer, she'd never pass . . ."

But of course I couldn't say that. So instead, I just held the scarf to Cat's skin and let her blood color the fabric, then my hand.

It wasn't until we pulled onto Hawthorne Boulevard, Cat's tree-lined street, that my mom finally spoke. "Is your mom home?" She pulled over in front of Cat's neighbor's house, a three-story Tudor that could probably fit our entire apartment in its garage.

Cat shook her head no.

"Your dad?"

No.

"Your little brother?"

"All a-a-at the s-soccer g-g-g-ame," Cat managed to say.

"Okay," my mom said. She smoothed back her blond hair—the color and texture of straw—and licked her lips. She eased the Honda into Cat's driveway and put it into park, but still left it running, probably because if she turned it off, it might never start again.

She got out of the car and came around to Cat's side, where she had to yank on the door—once, twice—before it would open. "C'mon, sweetie," she said to Cat, her voice honeyed with reassurance. She held out her hand, but Cat didn't move. *Take it,* I begged her silently. *My mom will say all the right things. She'll convince you this is all okay.* When Cat finally grasped Mom's fingers, I exhaled a little puff of breath and followed them into the house.

Within minutes, Mom had Cat in the downstairs bathroom, seated on the edge of the marble tub. She'd rummaged around for rubbing alcohol and tweezers, and was extracting the glass from Cat's skin. "It's fine, just fine," Mom kept saying over and over, like a mantra.

"See, Cat?" I imagined myself agreeing. "No biggie." But I didn't dare say anything—not with Cat's lower jaw thrust out like that, a mixture of anger and hurt on her face like I'd never seen. So instead I stayed frozen in the bathroom doorway, scared to get too close, scared of what Cat was thinking, scared of where this was all headed.

Cat's cut was deep and raw. If she needed stitches, there was no way Mom was going to say so. Her eyes were sharp as she cleaned out Cat's cut, put a huge gauze bandage on it, and taped everything down. She can sure snap out of a binge when she needs to, I thought.

"Okay, then," Mom said, leaning back on her heels. She patted Cat's knee like this had just been a scrape on the playground. "I know you're a little shaken up, but physically you're fine."

A corkscrew of Cat's black, curly hair fell into her face, but she didn't push it away. She just clenched her fists as Mom used the same reasoned tones she did when she was on the phone with the electric company or the landlord, trying to get our power back on or an extension on our rent. *It's all a misunderstanding, see? We're all good people here. Sometimes things happen, but that doesn't mean we need to go to any extremes. Right?*

"You should rest, take a nap, and maybe have some tea or something. You'll be fine. We're all fine." Mom stood and wiped her hands on her faded jeans. That was that.

Cat blinked like she was trying to process what my mom was saying. Like she was still trying to piece together how we'd gotten here—with blood spattered on her white tile floor and glass pieces clinking in her antique silver trash can. "Except," she said slowly, "except what about the other people back there? What if they were hurt? What if they needed help? You just drove away."

Cat's eyes found mine. "Jane," she said, like she was just now registering me standing in the doorway. Her teeth started clattering again. "Your f-f-face," she said. "You're cut too."

I put my hand up to my cheek and felt shards and dried blood against my fingertips. I jerked as if I'd touched a live electrical current.

"Jane's fine," my mom said, her skin illuminated from the gilded light above the vanity. It softened all her edges and angles, and she was so pretty just then, with the hollows in her cheeks filled out, and the shadows around her eyes nearly gone. She looked like she did after she came out of rehab a few years ago, actually. Not that her sobriety lasted.

Cat shook her head slowly, her shock beginning to fade. "No, she's not fine. *This* is not fine. It's not *okay*. You—you almost killed us. Because you were drunk. You picked us up and you drove the car *drunk*."

Mom's eyes flashed with fear, just for a moment. Her full, red lips paled. "No, honey. That's not it. We were in an accident, but everything's okay now. You're just shaken up is all."

Cat looked at me, and I swear to God she saw all the way *through* me—all the way down to that cold ball of fear anchored in the pit of my stomach. The fear that she understood the truth about what had gone down: that I *knew* the second we piled into the Honda that my mom was wasted. But rather than say anything, I'd let her drive us around drunk because speaking the truth out loud was so completely humiliating.

And now, here we were, post accident, and it was *all my fault.*

Cat stood and pushed past Mom, unbalancing her. Mom wobbled until she found the edge of the sink.

"Jane," Cat said, "this is crazy. This is so completely *insane.*" Cat touched my face like she was going to try and get some of the glass out, then dropped her hand.

All I could do was stare at her. Insane didn't even begin to cover it. "The only reason I'm not on the phone right now to the cops," Cat continued, "is for *you.*" She glanced at my mom, whose face was ashen. "But if I find out anyone is dead? I am turning your mom in. People—we could have—that truck almost . . ." She took a breath. "I know you cover for your mom all the time. And, fine, I'm going to do it too. This *once.* As long as no one died out there. Because I love you. Because you're my best friend. But never again, Jane. Do you understand me? If she ever comes within an inch of hurting me, or you, or anyone else again, I'm going to have the cops over here, and I'm going to get my dad's lawyers over here and make sure she gets locked up for as long as possible."

My mom let out her throaty everyone-is-getting-worked-up-over-nothing laugh. "Cat, honey—"

Cat wheeled around. Her heart-shaped face was hard with anger. "*Don't.* Don't you dare argue with me after what just *happened.* And after you had the nerve to ask me who's in my home so you can use it to clean me up in secret and hide what you *did.*"

My mom held up her hands. Her long nails arched over the top of her fingers. "Sweetie, calm down. This won't ge—"

"NO!" Cat stamped her foot. Her skin was crimson with cuts and anger. "You have a problem, Amanda. And you can't deal with it. So you know who deals with it? Jane. Don't think we don't see it. We *all* see it."

I wanted to sink down onto the cold tile and cover my ears.

"She comes to school exhausted every day. Why? Because she's up paying bills and working. She eats ramen noodles all the time because you're out spending money at the bar. You think my mom has her sleeping over here constantly just for fun? It's to get her away from *you*."

I tried to stop the tears rolling down my face because the salt stung the wounds in my cheeks and chin.

Cat turned back to me. "Enough with helping your mom," she said, her voice trembling. "Please, Jane. In the end, you're only making it worse. Okay? Do you hear me?"

I did the only thing I could do. I nodded, even though my mom was right there and we knew that if I didn't help her, we'd both be living out of the now-ruined back of the Honda.

"We're leaving," my mom said, brushing past Cat. The clack of her heels echoed like gunfire in the marbled bathroom. "Jane. Let's go." She held her head high as she walked through the foyer, out the front door. She didn't slam anything like I thought she would. She simply left.

"I'm so sorry," I whispered to Cat. It was the only thing I could think to say. We'd brought the hurricane of our lives into Cat's perfect house, and now we were taking off like we hadn't just torn everything up.

"Me too," Cat said, wiping away tears. "This is pretty fucked up."

I touched the glass in my cheeks. It was starting to feel hot. "I have to fix my face," I said.

Cat looked at me hard. "Jane. You have to fix your *life*."

Back at the Days Inn, I delete Cat's text and shove the phone into my pocket. I figure I'll write her later when I can get a better handle on my thoughts, when I can find some new way to tell her I'm doing fine down here. I'm fixing my life! And it's awesome!

Which is of course bullshit. Other than take some pictures, I haven't exactly done *anything*. At least not according to Cat's definition of what fixing my life means.

I hear the slam of a van door and see my brother walking by, carrying a laptop under one arm. His weight is mostly on the balls of his feet, meaning he moves quietly and quickly— the same way he did when we were kids and we had to sneak around the house without waking Mom up.

"Ethan," I say, and he stops like he's surprised to hear my voice. He slides his room card through the reader on the pool gate, then scrapes the legs of a chair across the concrete to sit next to me. The water's reflection paints him in giraffe prints of light.

"How are you feeling?" he asks, glancing at my head where the hailstone hit.

"Better," I say, studying Ethan's gray-blue eyes, the same as mine. We both have the same coarse, red-blond hair, same angular cheekbones and sharp jawline. On Ethan, the result is breathtaking—he could be a model if he wasn't a meteorologist. On me, the lines are too severe. I wish for more softness, more curves. But I'm bones and edges through and through. Just like Mom—physically, anyway.

I motion to the laptop. "Are you running the data? On today's chase?"

Ethan nods. "Even with Polly going down, we were still able to get some good measurements."

Most of the Torbros are PhD students at the University of Oklahoma, and their tornado work is funded through a grant. The goal for the summer is to use the grant money to document just about everything that happens around a tornado: temperature changes, wind speeds, barometric pressure readings, and other stuff I can barely get my mind around. With any luck, it will help them better understand how tornadoes form and why. Because, as common as they are, a lot about them is still a mystery.

Ethan rubs the bridge of his nose. I know this gesture—he does it when he's thinking hard. And no wonder. The Torbros aren't the only team out here doing this kind of work. There's hard-core competition from other chasers not just to get to the storms, but to figure out new ways to measure and study them. The team that's going to survive long term is the one that can get extra innovative and extra ballsy on chases, and at the same time figure out how to use the grant money as a bridge to something profitable and sustainable.

Which is where Polly comes in. She measures toxins and

pollutants in the air around a tornado, since the Torbros' theory is that the more toxins present in the atmosphere, the more a tornado can spin, and the more destructive it will be. With any luck, the Torbros will be able to use Polly to help predict a tornado's intensity based on how polluted the air around it is, then duplicate her technology and sell it to other chasers and researchers.

Ethan's fingers squeeze at the place where his nose meets his forehead. Another sign that he's deep in thought. Or stressed. Or both. It's been a long time since I've seen him do that. Last time we were together was two years ago. He came home for Christmas Day, then left the next morning. He said it was because he had research back at the lab that couldn't wait, but his tired frown and slumped shoulders told the truth: he was miserable at home. Which probably explains why he skipped town the minute he had his high school diploma, too. He barely waved as he roared away in his old Ford. He was eighteen when he fled; I was twelve.

Like he can sense my thoughts, Ethan clears his throat. "Seeing you get hurt today—it was tough. It made me realize that in the three weeks you've been down here, I've never told you how glad I am you made the trip."

I shift in my chair. I'm not used to the two of us having warm fuzzy moments.

"I've been trying to get you down here for ages, you know," Ethan continues. "And I meant what I said about you staying on after the season wraps. I know it's probably tough to think about, but I hope you'll consider it."

Tough to think about doesn't even begin to cover it. In the past, Mom hated when Ethan sent me e-mails asking me to come to Oklahoma and visit. "I'm so proud of everything he's been able to do," she'd say by way of qualifying what came next, "but *he* should really come to *us*. Family doesn't leave family. You shouldn't have to go down there and split us up even more." She'd freak if she knew he wanted me to come *live* with him.

"I will," I say. "I'll think about it." *On my own, by myself.* I don't add the last part only because Ethan will probably argue with me about how he understands better than anyone what life with Mom is like, even though he's been gone for *years*.

"You haven't said much about Mom and how things are with her," Ethan says, picking at the arm of the pool chair, "but if you want to talk about it, I'm here."

I swallow more irritation. I know he's trying to be helpful, and yeah, Ethan might not have walked out on us the way Mom likes to paint it, but he *did* leave. And now he suddenly wants to know how things are? Well, the way they are is great.

Awesome. Never better.

I stare at my fingernails. It's all lies, of course, but what am I supposed to tell him? About how we almost killed Cat? About how, right before I left, Mom peed in her own bed? *No one* needs to know that level of detail.

"I'm okay," I say, offering as little as possible. If I know to keep my mouth shut when arguing with a drunk, then I sure as heck have enough sense to keep it shut around a PhD student who could probably source a dissertation on what I had for breakfast.

"You could talk to someone else," Ethan offers. "If you didn't want to talk to me."

"Like who?"

Ethan shrugs. "Maybe just someone who's super experienced in this kind of stuff and who could really listen. And help."

I suddenly understand his meaning. "A shrink."

"A *professional*."

"Why do you seem to think there's so much wrong with me?" I ask.

Ethan exhales, probably willing himself to be patient. "It's not that I think there's anything wrong with you, per se. I think that the situation with Mom is messed up."

Messed up. The expression makes it sound like there are just a few things out of place here and there, which might describe most days with Mom, but not all of them. Certainly not the day I came home from school to find her passed out under our apartment building's bushes, topless. There were two neighborhood kids standing over her, taking pictures with their cell phones.

Messed up doesn't really do justice to the red spots of rage and humiliation that blinded me before I could scream at the kids to leave her alone and get the hell out of there. *Messed up* doesn't really cover the way the screaming didn't stop when I put my hands underneath her armpits and dragged her out of there—facedown, no less, so no one else would see her breasts. And *messed up* doesn't really describe how neighbors just shrugged it off, no one bothering to help us, because they'd been there, seen it, done it with the drunk lady and her daughter. Neither does *messed up* really convey the way I couldn't *stop* screaming, not even when we were back in the apartment, or the rawness at the back of my throat afterward that kept me hoarse for two days. Which was just as well, I suppose, because once my mom came to, I had no idea what to say to her.

How does Ethan expect me to talk to a stranger about that kind of stuff? I couldn't—*wouldn't*—because that's not how problems get fixed in my world. You just go through it. You deal with it. You survive one day and move on to the next.

"I'm not sure about the shrink thing," I say finally. "It's probably not for me."

Ethan nods. "Fair enough. But think about it, okay? It's been a rough year for you. And Mom. Speaking of which, how's Mom been handling the Uncle Pete thing?"

The black hole in my heart yawns. I struggle to close it, to neutralize the gravitational pull of my pain. Uncle Pete was my mom's brother, and he died this past winter by freezing to death in his car. He was a drug addict, and homeless, and we never talked to him much. But Mom took his death hard, blaming herself for it, telling me—and anyone else who would listen—that she should have done more to save him.

"That good, huh?" Ethan asks, studying my face.

"He was her *brother*," I say, more defensively than I mean to. "She's really upset." So much so that for these past few months, she'd started hitting Larry's, the neighborhood bar, hard. Not to mention the local party store. Since Uncle Pete died, the cost of her drinking has started to outweigh the cost of anything else in our house—even rent.

"She putting her pain into the bottle, then?" Ethan asks, as if my thoughts are just laid right there on the pool deck for him to read.

"Not really," I lie. "It was tough for a little bit, but now she's fine."

Ethan gives me this funny look like, *poor kid*, and I wonder if he thinks asking these questions, or having me around this summer, makes him *so* generous. Like he's *so* involved now or something. But really it's the least he can do, considering he gets a charmed life as a handsome researcher down here in Oklahoma and I'm trying to hold everything together back in Minnesota.

Except Ethan's on your side, I tell myself, remembering the time Ethan taught me to cook macaroni and cheese, and when he drove to the drugstore to get me tampons when I got my first period, even though his friend Trey worked there and might have seen him.

"Look," I say, "can we just drop this? Home is home. Here is here. Let's not mix the two, okay?"

Ethan runs a hand along the tanned back of his neck as if he's not quite sure about that idea. For a second, he looks like the *only* thing he wants is for those things to mix. But a moment later, he's eyeing the camera bag at my feet. "So, you want to go through your pictures from today and pick some to put up on the website?"

I nod, relieved that we're onto a different subject. I grab the camera, and Ethan scoots in closer. Together, we flip through the images on my small screen.

"This one's really good," he says, pointing at a picture of silvery leaves tossed by a wind gust. Afternoon light slants through the dust behind them.

"Thanks," I say, my heart swelling. The picture had been one of my favorites too, and secretly I like that Ethan's taking all this interest in my work.

"Whoa," Ethan says when we land on an image of him and Stephen running through a field, their bodies blurring as they bolt toward the black sky. "That's badass." The late-afternoon sun is igniting the other side of the horizon, putting everything in sharp contrast. Ethan's and Stephen's shadows are deep and dark—almost solid enough to be two more people. Ethan points at them. "It's like Ethan and Stephen Junior," he jokes.

"Too bad we left them out there," I reply. "I wonder if they got sucked up in the storm."

"They probably found a ditch and covered their heads."

"Oh, then I'm sure they were *fine*. I mean, what's a two-hundred-mile-per-hour wind gust when you have your head covered?"

Ethan grins. "Exactly."

We click through a few more images until a square-jawed motel employee rattles the pool gate. "This area is closed," he says, like he caught us drinking or partying, instead of just sitting here.

"Sorry," Ethan says, raising his hand in a half wave. "We'll be out of here in a minute." We collect our stuff as the motel Nazi watches. Lightning flashes in the distance, and Ethan pauses for a second to watch it.

"No matter how many times I see a storm," he says, "I can't get enough of them. Runs in the family, I guess."

"What, chasing?"

"No. Addiction."

I picture the mass of beer bottles in the recycling bin at home. I meant to haul them to the curb before I left, but didn't get around to it.

"I don't know about you," Ethan continues, "but I don't drink at all. If I go out, I'll have a Coke. That's it. Used to be I wouldn't even go near a bar, but I've mellowed in my old age." He winks at me, like joking about being twenty-three is hilarious.

Plenty of kids my age drink, but I'm like Ethan—I steer clear of it. I can't even stand to be the designated driver at parties, because carting around sloppy drunk kids is the opposite of a good time in my book. On the weekends, I'm usually over at Cat's, holed up in her basement watching movies.

"I know what we should do," Ethan says after a moment. "You and I should find something completely benign and get hooked on it."

"Like?"

"I don't know. How about butter?"

I can't help but giggle. "Maybe not. In large doses, it's pretty fatty."

"Insects?"

"Gross. How about shoes?"

"Too expensive," Ethan says, as we shuffle past the motel Nazi. "How about stamps?"

"Meh. Boring."

"Tiny dogs that never get any bigger than a hamburger?"

We're inside now, and my laughter bounces off the hallway's faded wallpaper and threadbare carpet. "Trained rabbits that can hunt and kill zombies?"

Ethan snorts. "Candy that never makes you fat but still tastes delicious?"

"Recyclable water bottles that automatically fill themselves?"

"Hamsters that can stop hurricanes?"

"That's the one," I say, sliding my motel card through my door reader. "That's the winning idea."

Ethan sighs, relieved. "Well, thank God. Now we can go to bed happy."

I hug him good night, wishing silently that was all it took.

3

The next morning, I'm up early to get breakfast at the motel's complimentary buffet before the Torbros hit the road on another chase. After packing up my small bag and cramming it with more free toiletries, I brush out my hair and place a vintage, feather-patterned headband just so on my head. It's beautiful—and the perfect thing to distract people from noticing my lame T-shirt that reads GO MILLERS! (courtesy of Minnetonka Mills High).

I pull my door shut behind me, thinking about how my mom put the headband on the kitchen table next to a glass of milk and a steak at six thirty in the morning, just days after the accident.

"What are you doing?" I'd asked when I'd dragged myself out of bed. Not only was Mom awake without me having to force her to get up, but she was dressed and cooking. In the gray morning light, her pale skin and yellow hair seemed ethereal— and I wondered for a minute if I was imagining her entirely.

"The gas works," she said, motioning to the stove, where another steak was sizzling. "Figure we should eat up what we can until they turn the power back on. I splurged and bought the meat for a special occasion, but I guess we'll just have it now. And look!" She opened up the cupboard underneath the sink and pulled out a bag of tea lights. Her eyes sparkled. "Got them at the dollar store. We can add ambience!"

She placed a few of them around the kitchen and immediately the room was transformed. The cold edges were replaced by a soft, warm glow. "Isn't it romantic, *dahling*?" she asked, and I laughed, giddy with the improbability of all of it. "Go on, eat," she said, pointing to the steak, and that's when I saw the headband.

"What's this?" I asked, picking up the arc of soft feathers.

"Found it at a garage sale and knew you had to have it. I know you love those old fashions."

It's more like when you're broke, you get good at figuring out how to have a sense of style for cheap, which usually means buying old, old stuff. Not that I was going around dressed like a flapper or anything. Mostly I spent what little money I had on a hint of flair here or there. A scarf. A bracelet. One time I found a pair of fur-trimmed satin shoes from the 1940s at a Salvation Army. Because if I was going to have to wear castoffs, the least I could do was jazz them up. Last season's crappy hoodies from Target looked way better when you stuck a faux Depression glass pin on them.

"It's beautiful," I said, stroking the feathers. "Thank you."

My mom plunked down next to me at our battered table—

the one with toilet paper shoved under two of its legs to keep it from wobbling. "Let's eat these steaks," she said. "It'll be like a picnic. And then you can get in the shower before they turn off the water, too."

We smiled at each other, then ate the steaks like it was totally normal to be gnawing on a slab of beef before school. While we chewed, we talked about my mom's coworkers at the women's clinic where she works, and about our neighbor Mr. Eisengrath, who went for a walk the other day in nothing but his robe.

And this is what I thought the whole time we were sitting there talking: *My mom is not like other moms.* It was the most awesome truth in the world right then. Because, okay, fine, the power's off, but so what? My mom is young, and she's beautiful, and we're hanging out and talking like friends, which we are. And we're having a super unconventional breakfast because we're trying to make the best of things. Together. Her and me. Us versus the world.

You don't go through things with people and not love them more for it. It's like those guys in the army who fight in muddy trenches and drag each other out of harm's way and are blood brothers for life because of it all. Only in our case, my mom and I faced eviction notices and power shutoffs together.

We talked about the free concert we could go see that weekend and whether it would snow again, even though it was May, but in Minnesota there was always a chance.

But the one thing we didn't talk about was the accident.

Not once did we bring up how we'd turned on the news for three nights in a row, biting our nails and watching the screen, wondering if someone had died out there on the roads (no one had). Not once did we mention the cuts on my face that I was covering with makeup, or the Honda, battered and crunched in the apartment's parking lot, dripping oil onto the blacktop like blood. But still running—somehow, thank God.

And we didn't talk about Cat.

"Are you babysitting tonight?" my mom asked, sweeping the dishes into the sink when we were all finished.

"Yeah," I replied, "for the Bargers."

"Oh, good," she said. "Anyone else lined up?"

"The Clydes asked for Sunday night, but I have a test on Monday so I'm not—"

"Oh, you can manage it," my mom said, pushing my hair back to kiss my forehead. "Can't you?"

I poked at some of the toilet paper under the table with my toe. "I guess. But you just got paid last Friday, right? We can't need money that badly already. I only paid the cell phone bill online so we should have—"

"There you go again, Mr. Scrooge!" she laughed. "Being so tight with the funds all the time."

"I can't be tight with it when it just disappears," I say.

"Funny," she says giggling like this is all a big joke.

"Did you spend it all at Larry's again?" I pressed. "Is that where it went?" Lodged in my throat was the *real* question I wanted to ask, which is whether or not Mom was getting into something bigger, maybe speed or meth, because we were just so broke all the time. Surely she wasn't drinking enough to bankrupt us, was she?

"Not all of it. But I had a couple baby showers at work. Donna invited me to lunch, and I splurged on the steaks. I promise I'll be more careful next time. If you'll just babysit for the Clydes, we'll be fine. I'm sure of it."

I nodded. I wanted to believe her. "I guess so."

Mom picked up one of the tea lights and blew it out. "I need to run, gotta get to the clinic early today. You'll handle cleaning up?"

I took in the grease splatter around the stove and the little tea lights, some tipped over, wax dripping down the counters and onto the linoleum floor. What had looked romantic twenty minutes ago was more like a crime scene now.

"No problem," I said anyway, because I didn't want to spoil the mood.

My mom smiled. "Thanks, honey." She gave me one more kiss before heading out the door. I watched her go, heard the clatter of the Honda shuddering to life, and told myself she really was going in to work early. There was no way—not after the accident—that she'd be stopping for a forty of Coors before work.

Just to be sure, I peeked out the front window and looked down at Hyde Street, watching my mom turn left out of the apartment complex. My heart sank because her work was the opposite way. But there *was* a party store just down the road in the direction she'd headed.

I made my way back to the kitchen, trying to decide what to do. The answer, as usual, was a big fat nothing. I couldn't call her and ask her what she was up to; she'd flat-out lie. I couldn't call her work and tell them she'd been drinking; they'd fire her and then we *really* wouldn't be able to pay our bills. I couldn't tell anyone at school because, in the end, they'd probably call some state agency, and *no way* was that an option.

Suddenly, there was a reckless beating inside of me, like a trapped bird's wings. For a second I thought I was having a heart attack until I realized—it was fear. The beating quickened, and I felt as if the glass from the accident was pumping through my bloodstream.

There's no time for this, I thought. I gritted my teeth and fought the emotion, struggled upstream against it. *Do something. Stay busy. Don't stop.*

I had to start cleaning. I took a breath, figuring I could tackle the kitchen for about fifteen minutes before I'd have to get in the shower and head for school. But when I went to run the water for the dishes, there was only the wheeze and groan of empty pipes.

The water had been shut off, too.

Think. Keep going.

I grabbed my backpack, which always had a change of clothes and a toothbrush in it. If I got to school early enough, I could shower there. I pulled out my wallet for bus money, and my mouth dried up when I realized it was empty.

I'd had ten dollars in there yesterday.

My mom had taken it.

I opened the cupboard above the coffeemaker to check the change bowl, but that was empty, too.

I checked my phone for the time. At least my cell was still working, thank God. It was 7:16, which meant the (free) school bus I could catch three blocks down had left ten minutes ago.

The birds' wings wanted to come back, but I forced myself to relax. *No use in getting stressed. You're the problem solver. You can do this. You always figure out a way.*

Cat could come get me, I reasoned after a while. Cat's mom let her borrow the car when it was important. This qualified, right? She could pick me up, and once I got to school, I might not have time to shower, but I could at least wash my face and brush my teeth.

Cat.

I juggled my cell in my hand. We hadn't talked much since the accident. I mean, we'd talked—like in the hallways and stuff at school—but we hadn't *talked* talked. Not like before, when we'd just chat about anything and everything in our easy way because that's what best friends do.

I scrolled to Cat's number. She answered on the third ring.

"Hey, you," she said, like she was forcing herself to sound glad to hear from me.

"Hey, Cat," I replied. "I don't mean to be a total pain here, but I'm kinda stuck without a ride to school. I was wondering if you could come get me."

Cat paused. "Where's your mom?"

"She left for work already," I said. "The clinic's having a free vaccination day, and she had to get there early to set up."

The lie left my lips so easily. Why did I do that? Why couldn't I just leave it at "she had to work early"?

Cat grunted. She wasn't buying it. "No money for the bus?" she asked.

"No."

"Huh. You're still babysitting all the time, though, right?"

My jaw clenched. So this is how it's going to be, I thought. Cat gets to bust my balls because of the accident. And I just have to take it.

"What do you want me to say?" I asked finally. "What am I supposed to do?"

Cat didn't respond. My heart froze, and I worried she'd hung up on me. Then I heard a sniff and realized she was crying. "I'm sorry, Jane," she said. "I don't mean to be a bitch. I don't. I know your mom has a problem . . ." She trailed off. I swallowed down the lump in my own throat.

Tears are just eye pee, I could hear my mom saying, *and nobody likes it when you piss your face.*

I blinked to hold them back.

"I'll come get you," Cat said, "but we're not going to school. We have to talk. Okay?"

I nodded, even though Cat couldn't see it. "Okay."

I hung up and waited in the dark, dirty kitchen for Cat to come get me.

4

My sandals hardly make a sound on the lobby's stained carpet as I approach the breakfast room. But even if they did, I wouldn't be able to hear it above the cacophony of the Torbros arguing.

I round the corner to see them bent over a table, studying the radar on Mason's laptop, trying to figure out where to chase today.

"There is no way we should go that far south when we've got dry lines right here," Hallie says, pointing at the computer screen. "They look better than the ones that are farther away."

Victor scoffs. "Remind me again why we should listen to someone who learned weather by watching Al Roker?" He pushes his lanky black hair out of his eyes and glares at Hallie. His ugly scar makes him look even angrier, and I mentally give Hallie full props for not backing away from him.

"Enough," Stephen says. "Insults won't be tolerated, Victor. Watch your tone." Stephen stands to his full height. He hasn't shaved since we've been down here, and right now his beard makes it seem like there's even *more* of him, if that's possible. If I were Victor, I'd reverse a few steps, but of course Victor doesn't, probably because he's older than Stephen and, somewhere in his brain, still thinks he's the boss.

"What, so you're on her side now?" Victor asks, his dark eyes blazing.

"This isn't about sides," Ethan interjects. "It's about our team. It's about *science*."

"Screw off, Boy Scout," Victor replies. "No one asked you."

"Vic," Stephen says, lowering his voice, "please stop. No one wants to see you acting like this."

"Then fine," Victor says, collecting his cell phone and a few miscellaneous papers, "I'm *gone*."

He storms past me without so much as a glance.

"I take it Victor's permanently constipated, then?" Mason asks. He's still got the duct tape in his freckled hand, mid tear—he was fixing a walkie-talkie when the fighting broke out.

"I'm sorry, you guys," Stephen says, hunching his shoulders. "Victor hasn't been the same since . . . well, you know."

The same since what? I wonder, approaching the table.

"I know he's exceptionally hard to deal with right now," Stephen continues, "but he's also an integral member of this team. He understands Polly better than anyone, and we need him. He'll get over this thing. I know he will."

I'm about to ask what part of the story I'm missing, when Hallie spots me and speaks first.

"Oh, hey, Jane," she says. She looks adorable in a cowboy

hat, shorts, and rugged boots that come to just above the ankle. She's not even posing about the Western thing—she actually grew up on a ranch in Texas. Her blond hair, like mine except silky and straight and without the hints of red—which is to say, nothing like mine at all—is pulled into a low ponytail.

"Hey," Ethan says to me. "You sleep okay?"

"Sure," I say quickly, wanting to circle back to Victor. "Everything okay here?"

"Yeah, yeah," Stephen says, waving his hand like he's ready to wipe away the whole discussion. "Victor just needs to get with the program."

"So we chase the nearby dry lines today?" Hallie asks, speaking again before I can get any questions out.

"Absolutely," Stephen says, and I rack my brain to remember what the heck a dry line is. After a moment, it occurs to me that it's the line where hot air meets cold air, which is what needs to happen for twisters to form.

Mason, Ethan, Hallie, and Stephen are all back to discussing the radar, which is my cue to grab food, though I make a mental note to ask Ethan about Victor later.

I head toward the waffle maker, passing the coffee and juice machines. This early in the morning, I practically have the whole buffet to myself. But just as I get there, someone's standing next to me. "You using the waffle maker, or can I go?"

I look over and am surprised to see a guy around my age. There just aren't that many teenagers at an Oklahoma Days Inn on a Thursday morning. I'm about to ask him what he's doing here when he points to the waffle machine. "Seriously. Can I use this? I'm starving."

He taps his foot a little. He's wearing the same brand of shirt Cat bought for her boyfriend last Christmas. Designer crap, meaning he's probably some rich kid who thinks he's entitled to waffles before everyone else. Most likely he's just passing through Oklahoma on a road trip. His douchebag frat friends are probably only seconds from showing up.

"Whatever," I say, holding back an eye roll only because, with his tan skin and dark hair, this guy isn't terrible looking. The next thing I know, he's ladling out the batter in messy, drippy globs that drive me nuts.

Before I can get any more irritated, I hit the fruit and cereal. I settle with my breakfast at a table by myself, fork a pear slice, and try to enjoy the peace and quiet, since it's such a change from meals at home. I know I should be loving the fact that I have as much food as I want, that the water will come out of the tap anytime I need it to, that I'll have electricity when I flip a switch. Plus Ethan's paying me every week for my photos, and no one's stealing my money.

I should be happy, but the truth is, I can barely get breakfast down my throat. Nothing about this feels right. No way should I be down here enjoying free food while my mom flies solo at home. What will *she* eat? I wonder if she's checked her voice mail or remembered to cut the dryer sheets in half to make them last longer.

It's fine, I tell myself. I take a deep breath. But the air expanding inside my lungs doesn't calm me down much. And the ache in my chest is getting worse. I glance around the breakfast room, wondering what I can do. Maybe I can bring Hallie some coffee. Or help Mason organize all his equipment.

Except everyone seems just fine. No one needs me to do that stuff, which, if you asked Cat, she'd say is a good thing. But she wouldn't understand it's a *hard* thing, too.

No, Cat would just shake her head, like she did the day she came to pick me up from the apartment before school.

"You're trying to keep it together, I know you are, but it's like nailing Jell-O to the wall," Cat said as we settled on the worn sofa in my living room, ignoring the fact that we were both going to get detention for not showing up at school on time. I tried not to stare at the gash above Cat's eyebrow, which was covered with a smaller bandage now, but still very much there. She caught me looking and touched the dressing self-consciously.

"My mom and dad think you and I crashed our bikes," she said. It had been months since Cat and I went anywhere on two wheels. I'm relieved they bought it. "I told them you were hurt too, but I probably didn't even need to say anything. You just have those red marks. You could pass them off as zits or something."

It was my turn to touch my face. The skin was hot where my fingers landed. Probably from guilt since Cat would no doubt have a scar from all this, while I just had cuts that were already fading.

"It was a stupid cover, I know," Cat continued, watching me. "But the thing is, I'm not as good a liar as you are."

She let the words hang there for a moment. I imagined grabbing each letter—L-I-A-R—and shoving them all into the trash. But of course that was impossible and, besides, Cat was right. I *did* lie. She just couldn't seem to understand that this is the way it had to be. I didn't have any other choice.

"But it's not even the lies that upset me so much," Cat continued. "The worst part of this all is, you're not actually helping your mom. You're hurting her, and eventually, someone is going to die if you don't change. Whether it's your mom from liver failure, or someone she runs over while drunk. Either way, you won't be blameless next time. Not unless you figure something out."

"Fine, but what am I supposed to *do*?" I asked, thinking Cat had some nerve coming in here with her hundred-dollar backpack and her mom's Lexus parked outside, telling me how to live a life she'd completely fail at after a day. Granted, the accident was awful, and I did play a part in it. But still. What kind of twisted form of intervention was this, when I wasn't the one with the drinking problem?

Cat pulled out a crumpled sticky note from her pocket. Her hands were shaking as she unfolded it. She cleared her throat. "Stop calling in to work for her, saying she's sick," she said, reading off the paper, which was covered in her tiny, bubbly writing. She'd made a *list*, for crying out loud. "Stop allowing her to take your babysitting money. Stop paying bills. Do not

41

tell any lies, period, to cover for her." She took a breath. "*Do* tell a counselor at school what's going on. *Do* start attending Al-Anon meetings. And *do* come live with me if you want to. Or go live with someone else. School lets out in a couple weeks, and you should be somewhere else for the summer. But—and this is the last one—*do* let your mom hit bottom, so she can realize she needs professional help and sobriety."

Cat shoved the note back into her pocket and looked at me. I expected her to be teary again, but her eyes were clear. Her chin was up. "So?" she asked. "What do you think?"

I took a breath. My heart was pounding, though I couldn't say why. Cat was clearly wrong about everything, so it wasn't like I didn't have a leg to stand on. And, it's not like I was mad at her—she was just doing what she thought best. So why was I getting all emotional?

"You're my best friend," I began, "and I don't know what I'd do without you. I'm so super sorry about the accident. It was awful, and I never should have let us get into that car. But I don't think it means you understand any of the stuff that my mom and I go through. If I do those things on your list, my mom will lose her job. We'll get evicted, and we'll have nowhere to go. My mom will still have a problem—but in your version she'll have it in the back of the Honda instead of in an apartment."

Cat opened her mouth, but I barreled forward. "I know things with my mom are fucked up. I'm not arguing that point. But until you're *in* it, until you live it, you can't sit there and say what it's going to take to fix it. I'm sorry, but you can't."

Cat tucked a piece of hair behind her ear. She nodded. "All

right, then. Here's the bottom line. I love you. And it's because I love you that you need to know that I can't be friends with you if you don't try to at least do *something* on this list." She pulled the paper back out from her pocket and put it on the coffee table, then stood. "I'm sorry. But I can't be friends with you if this is how it's going to be."

I stood too. My heart was jackhammering now, and I could feel my face flush. "Wait, so suddenly you're dumping me?"

Cat looked at the list. "Unless something changes."

"Unless I do your chores, you mean. And, for the record, that's manipulative. Not to mention ridiculous."

"No," Cat said, marching over to the light switch and flicking it over and over to no effect, "*this* is ridiculous." She went to the coffee table and grabbed the television remote. She hit the power again and again. "*This* is ridiculous," she said when it didn't turn on. She went to the sink, lifted the faucet, and let the pipes groan. "*That* is what's fucked up, Jane."

"Okay!" I said, wanting her to stop. "Okay, you made your point already. Little miss house-on-the-hill, can-I-have-a-convertible-for-my-birthday has made her point."

Cat froze. "This has nothing to do with where I live or what I drive. My parents love you. They want you to stay with us, okay? It's not about money."

"Fine," I said. "Whatever."

"So that's it?" Cat asked. "*Whatever*?"

"That's it," I replied.

Cat stared at me for a moment before she shook her head and walked to the door.

"Don't forget your list on the way out," I said.

She didn't even look at me. "Keep it," she replied, and pulled the door closed.

And that was that.

At least it was until I decided to spend the summer in Oklahoma with my brother.

It was one of the things on her stupid list, which I'd lifted off the coffee table and buried in the middle of a book at the back of my shelf. I couldn't say exactly why I kept it around, except that a hazy, gnawing feeling was pulling at me, telling me Cat might not know everything, but she might know *something* I didn't. Which is why I texted her when I had news:

Am leaving 2 live w Ethn in Oklhma 4 summer.

Radio silence for an hour. Then finally, a text back:

Im prd of u.

I nearly drop my pear when the chair next to me is suddenly occupied. "Are you with the Torbros?" It's Waffle Boy. I want to be annoyed, but I'm too caught off guard by him—and the fact that his waffle looks like it's been massacred, then laid to rest in a syrup-and-whipped-cream grave.

"Um, yeah," I reply, working simultaneously to stop thinking about Cat and to figure out how this random rich kid knows who the Torbros are.

"Cool," he says, and shoves a mass of carbs and stickiness into his mouth. While he chews, he studies me with green eyes that are like a mixture of sunlight and moss. His dark brown hair juts out in every direction and should look ridiculous—but somehow doesn't. A current vibrates through every vertebra on my spine. It's all I can do not to shiver.

When a guy in a burgundy shirt and khakis strides by, Waffle Boy raises a hand, flagging him down. Like it's a restaurant, and this guy is a *waiter* or something. "Hey, yeah, I was wondering if we could get more strawberries at the breakfast buffet?" Waffle Boy asks.

The guy shakes his head and gives a little wave, the kind like when you're saying no thanks to a second helping. "I don't work here," he says, and walks on.

Unbelievable, I think. Waffle Boy must have people waiting on him all the time if he's picking people out of a crowd and thinking they should bring him stuff.

"My bad," Waffle Boy says. "He's wearing the same colors as the front desk guys." He laughs in an easy way, unfazed, and I think that if I'd just done that in front of a stranger, I'd be ducking my head, red from embarrassment.

I stare at the box of Cheerios in front of me. I want to leave, but I can't think of how to exit gracefully.

"Cool headband," Waffle Boy says. "You make that yourself?"

I shake my head. "No. It's vintage."

"Nooo?" he draws out the word with a smile. "I've never heard it pronounced like that. Where are you from?"

"Minnesota."

"Oh. Yah. Minnesota, eh?"

I bristle. It sounds like he's making fun of me. "What's wrong with the way I talk?"

"No, nothing. Sorry. It's just very . . . *Fargo*."

"Fargo's in North Dakota," I reply as he swallows down more bites.

"Yeah. I mean, I was talking about the movie, but. Okay."

My stomach falls at the flat note in his voice. This kid might be a little . . . entitled, but he's not horrible. I don't have to be mean. Cat says I get bitchy around cute boys because I'm nervous.

"Wh—where are you from?" I venture, lightening up.

"Vermont." He's all smiles again, and I swear, it's like his mouth is plugged into a light socket it's so bright. "I'm doing an internship with the Twister Blisters."

I sit back, surprised. Waffle Boy is decidedly *not* on a rich-kid road trip.

Even someone like me knows the Twister Blisters are the rock stars of tornado chasing. They roll around in Escalades and have Weather Network cameras on them for almost every chase. Their founder, Alex Atkins, was just on the cover of *Time*. "Are they—are the Twister Blisters *here*?"

Waffle Boy jerks his head. "Next door at the Motel 6."

"Then shouldn't you be over there too? Being their intern and all?" Great, now I'm using words that sound like I want him to get up and walk away. But I don't. Not really.

"Don't tell, but sometimes I hit a nearby motel to get away from the filming. And the egos." He places his hands six inches from either ear and puffs out his cheeks.

"Big heads, huh?" I ask, biting back a smile because this guy's suddenly borderline adorable.

He nods. "The first week I was with them, they actually

tried to tell me that bringing them breakfast in bed was part of my job. I ignored the order and almost got fired, but then they wouldn't have had anyone to lug around the heavy equipment." I glance at his callus-free hands and figure maybe lugging is a new thing for him. "Are the Torbros the same way to you?"

"Oh, I'm not an intern. I mean, I'm a photographer. I'm taking pictures for the Torbros website. My brother, Ethan McAllister? He's a researcher with them."

"Yeah?" Waffle Boy's eyebrows shoot up like he's actually interested. "I've totally seen that site. The photo gallery is amazing. Super professional."

I feel my face heat up with the compliment. "Thanks."

Waffle Boy holds out a banana. "I'm Max, by the way," he says, like I should shake hands with his yellow fruit. The intensity of his eyes is like a lightning bolt striking too close. I can feel the electricity of it.

"I'm Jane." I don't shake the banana.

"Well, then," he says. "Jane." He starts unpeeling the banana. "Nice to meet you."

He chews, and my brain becomes a white sheet. I fumble for words. Any words. "I was hit by hail yesterday," I say suddenly. I want to melt. I know I sound stupid.

To my surprise, Max laughs. "I got cow shit on my shoe on Sunday," he says. "We were in a field watching a wall cloud."

This time I can't hide the smile. I'm about to tell him that last week Ethan kept farting in the van so much, we had to open every single window, but just then, a cluster of guys enters the breakfast lounge. There are six of them, and they're all wearing jeans and embroidered polo shirts with the same logo: THE TWISTER BLISTERS.

"Crap," Max mutters. "The dick parade is here."

I watch as two cameramen trail in after, rolling tape. "And, look," Max says. "They brought their balls."

5

The second the Twister Blisters and the camera crew saunter into the breakfast room, Stephen and Ethan both stand. The Twister Blisters might be on TV, but Stephen and Ethan are the ones that look like movie stars. Well, maybe more Ethan than Stephen right this minute, since Stephen looks a lot like Brad Pitt during his scary facial hair phase. But still.

I spot the Blisters' founder, Alex Atkins, right away. He's smaller in real life.

Alex holds out a hand, and Stephen takes it. "How's your season so far?" Alex asks. I wonder if he's smirking for the camera or if he always looks like that much of a dick. "Heard you got caught in some hail yesterday."

"We got out just in time," Stephen says. "And you? How are things?"

"Good. All good," Alex says, reminding me suddenly of the vintage Harry Houdini posters Cat's little brother has in his room. Small but compact, Alex looks like he might be able to weasel out of a lot of dangerous situations. He motions to the cameras. "The Weather Network is on our tail almost every chase. Got some new equipment from them, so we don't have to build gear with duct tape in the hotel rooms at night." His eyes shift to Mason, and he snickers. Apparently Alex has no problem with appearing like a total jerkwad on national television.

My brother raises his eyebrows. "Remind me again, Alex. How many tornadoes have you guys seen this season?" One of the camera guys adjusts his angle so he has a better view of Ethan.

The room goes quiet. I sneak a glance at Max, who has his tongue poked into his cheek.

"None, yet. But the season's barely started."

"Huh," Ethan says. "We've already seen two."

One of the Twister Blisters whistles at Ethan. "Is that a challenge? Because it sounds like a challenge."

"It can sound like whatever you want it to. I'm just pointing out the facts."

Alex laughs, but there's no humor in it. "Since you're so good at *pointing things out,* Ethan, then maybe you can point out Stephen's brother." Alex looks around the room. "Where's Victor? I don't see him here. He wouldn't be . . . *afraid* to show up for work, would he?"

More crap about Victor. What is going on with that guy?

Stephen's face darkens, but it's Ethan who speaks. "Our team is just fine, Alex. All of us. And *all* of us are going to have a blast kicking your ass in the chases this summer."

"You can't touch us," Alex says, like he knows our equipment is on the fritz. Like he knows our van is rusted and needs new tires, and the grant money we've scraped together for the season barely covers food and lodging.

Ethan shrugs. The camera hasn't moved from him. "Why not? Let's see who can catch the most twisters this season. Or get the closest to one. What do you say, Stephen?"

Stephen's face is still cloudy, and I wonder what he'll do. Stephen might not be the oldest Torbro (at twenty-seven, Victor's got that honor), but he's been chasing for way longer than anyone else on the team. Among the Torbros there's a rumor that Stephen's first word as a baby was *atmosphere*. Whatever happens is his call.

"Loser cleans out the winner's van at the end of the season," Stephen says after a moment. "And buys the whole group dinner."

I almost shudder. I can only imagine what the inside of the Twister Blisters vans look like after an entire summer of chasing.

"Those stakes seem a little tame," Alex says. "I say we raise them."

Ethan's eyes narrow. "In what way?"

"We win, we get the blueprints for Polly."

Stephen harrumphs. "*Never.*"

"You win, you get the Weather Network."

Even the camera operators look up from their lenses to see what Ethan and Stephen will say to *that*.

"You can't guarantee the Weather Network," Hallie says,

chiming in after a moment. "You don't *own* the network. You can't tell them which chase teams to follow."

Alex's eyes drag slowly over Hallie's body, up and down. Flames of anger light my insides when I see that. Hallie is a kick-ass chaser and an even better scientist. She also happens to be five-ten, with a completely banging body. It totally sucks right now that all Alex and the Blisters—and no doubt the cameras—can see is her looks.

"I don't own the Weather Network, it's true," Alex says, "but I *am* an executive producer. And I absolutely do get a say in who the network follows on chases. Especially next season. The field's wide open."

In three steps, Hallie is standing in front of Alex, towering over him, even though his cowboy boots have a heel on them. "No way," she says. "You're full of crap. There is no chance in hell the Weather Network made you an executive producer."

Alex stares into Hallie's brown eyes and doesn't back down. "Is this a bet within a bet?" he asks. He gestures to the cameraman on his left, never taking his eyes off Hallie. "Ask him. If he confirms I'm an executive producer, you have dinner with me. If not, *I* have dinner with *you*."

"Ha-ha, very funny, Alex," Hallie says, her voice flat. "But I think I'd rather hang out at that pig farm in the next county over."

"Probably Alex's mom is over there," Mason chimes in. Next to me, Max guffaws so loudly that the camera lens finds us, and I look at the floor, mortified to be anywhere near their footage.

"It's true," the cameraman says as he pans away from us, finally, and back to Alex. "Alex Atkins is an executive producer at the Weather Network."

"Good for him, then," Hallie says. "But I'd still rather hang out at the pig farm."

Alex ignores her and refocuses on Stephen and Ethan. "So deal or no deal, boys? Polly if we chase more twisters or get close enough to lose our shirts in an updraft, and the network if you do. What do you say?"

I can almost feel the dilemma tangling my brother's brain. If next season they could have Polly *and* the network on them, they'd be the new A-listers of chasing. They might have better equipment too—after all, who knows what the network might give them, especially considering the Escalades parked at the next motel over.

But if they lost, they'd lose *big*. The cameras wouldn't be such a hard defeat, since they never really had them in the first place. But losing Polly? They'd forfeit their edge, the technology that could set them apart. Losing Polly could mean losing *everything*.

Stephen raises an eyebrow at Ethan. "What do you think?" he says.

Ethan takes a breath, and right then, I know. This is going to be like the time Mom told him that he couldn't get all B's on his report card and, the next semester, he brought home all A's. This is going to be like the time Tommy Letrowski boasted he could hold his hand over a candle for five seconds, and Ethan said he could do it for fifteen, and even though his flesh bubbled and smelled like charred barbecue, he didn't once move it.

"We should do it," Ethan says. "We got this."

"All right," Stephen agrees.

"Oh, just one more thing," Alex says, before anyone can shake on the bet. "I think we should ensure the chase teams stay as intact as possible for the bet. If anyone from one of the teams goes AWOL, so to speak, that team forfeits automatically. Deal?"

I look at Max, who shrugs, clearly as confused as I am. Stephen's hands clench, like he wants to grab Alex's jugular and start squeezing at any moment.

"Fine," Ethan says quickly. "Whatever." He extends his hand. Alex grins and shakes it. Alex offers his hand to Stephen, who pauses long enough to have everyone shifting uncomfortably. Finally, they shake.

"Gonna be a hell of a season," Alex says, heading for the door.

The cameras are still rolling when they leave the room.

Rather than watch the Twister Blisters and their TV crew file out, I put my back to the scene, my insides heavy. That felt . . . gross. Like I was watching a corrupt deal go down in a back alley or something. It was also completely confusing. I have no idea what the part about the teams remaining intact meant.

Max elbows me. "If you're worried about the bet, don't sweat it. Alex has been spending more time lately fixing his hair than plotting storm courses. It means we're missing tornadoes."

"Really?"

"Really. And Alex might be a Weather Network executive producer, but that doesn't mean the Twister Blisters are the only game in town. I heard one of the guys in our group saying the network's considering covering the Hail Yeahs too. *This season.*"

"Thanks," I say to Max. He's trying to be encouraging, which is sweet of him. Not to mention Max's face is open and kind, and right then I think it's too bad he's interning for the Twister Blisters and not the Torbros.

We both get to our feet. "It was nice meeting you," he says.

"You too." I find myself meaning it.

"Probably I'll see you around. If Alex ever pulls his head out of his butt, maybe we'll be chasing the same storm one of these days."

"Totally." I want to say more, but my vocabulary has disappeared.

Max gives me a wave and heads back to the Motel 6. While the Torbros collect their laptops and power cords, I stack the dishes on the table and wipe it down. I'm glad my suitcase is already zipped up and ready to go.

If we can locate Victor, my guess is we'll be out chasing ten minutes from now.

6

Somewhere north of Wichita, we pull off Highway 96 and into a two-pump gas station. I jump out of the van, and dust billows at my feet.

The bright afternoon sun glints off a rusted Texaco sign. Across the street is another gas station—but it's boarded up. Next to that is a small brick church with a sign that reads GIVE THE LORD YOUR TROUBLES. HE CAN TAKE THEM!

Mason hops out of the van behind me. "Another beautiful day in beautiful Kansas!" he says, spreading his arms wide. His freckled skin is borderline reflective in the afternoon light. "There's a bright golden haze on the meadooow!" he sings. He motions to the flat road like it's a rolling wheat field.

"Are you seriously going to sing *Oklahoma!* in every state?" Hallie asks, coming around from the other side of the van.

"Why not?" Mason asks. "It's a classic. Say you throw *Oklahoma!* and *Cats* into a twister. Only one can survive. I pick *Oklahoma!* every time."

"Because *Cats* sucks," Hallie says. "Say you throw *Oklahoma!* and *Lord of the Rings* into a twister. Only one can survive. Which is it?"

"Dur," says Mason. "*Lord of the Rings.* But that's an awful setup for the vortex game. The decisions are supposed to get increasingly difficult, not easier."

"But *some* people might pick *Oklahoma!* over *Lord of the Rings,*" I say.

"Some insane people," Mason replies. "Worst round of the vortex game ever." He wipes his forehead—already turning pink in the sun—and heads toward the gas station convenience store. "I need a beef stick."

"Ah, the vortex game," Hallie says. "So ridiculous, only a chaser would love it." On the other side of the van, Ethan's using an ancient gas pump to fill the tank. The numbers are the old-fashioned kind, not digital, so you can actually hear a click as the price goes up and up.

"I'm not even sure I *understand* the vortex game," I confess. "What's the deal again?"

"The way your brother explained it to me when I started playing last season is that you're supposed to picture a twister out on the plains. And say you know it's going to suck up two things. Your cat or your homework, maybe. Only one is going to survive the encounter. Which do you pick?"

"The cat," I answer, even though my mom and I don't have any pets.

"Okay," Hallie nods. "Now put the cat up against something else. Something you'd have a harder time letting go of.

The cat and the six-hundred-dollar emerald earrings you got from a secret admirer, maybe."

"I don't have a secret admirer," I say, thinking that Hallie—with her Bambi-brown eyes and her long legs—must have a thousand of them.

"Well, whatever the choices are, I guess you're supposed to learn something about yourself with every decision you make," Hallie says. "Ideally, at the end of the game, because you've discovered so much about yourself, you'll be able to know which decision to make when you put two huge showstoppers up against each other. It's like chaser theology or something. Chaser dogma."

I'm about to ask Hallie which she'd pick if Victor or Alex Atkins were sucked up into a tornado, when my cell phone erupts with my mom's ring. "Sorry," I apologize, pulling it out. "I have to take this."

"No problem."

Desperate for a place where I can talk privately, I duck behind a rusted truck at the back of the building.

"Hi, Mom."

"Hi, Janey. How's my favorite storm chaser? Have you caught any tornadoes today?"

She says it like they're all over the place and we just have to rope one into the van.

"I'm good. We're in Kansas right now and hoping to get a twister before the day's out. Stephen thinks we have a good shot."

"Which one's he again?"

"The founder. Big guy? Deep voice?"

"Of course. I'm so proud of you, honey. I tell everyone how you're taking award-winning pictures down in Tornado Alley. I showed the girls at work that link you sent me. Your pictures were right there. I knew they were yours the second I spotted them, they were so beautiful."

I stare at the few tough blades of grass at my feet. "Thanks. But they're not *actually* award-winning or anything. They're just up on the Internet."

"You taking them with the camera I got you?" she asks. She's talking about last year when she gave me a camera for my birthday. She told me she'd squirreled away money for months to buy it for me. Tears had rolled down my face then, because as tight as things were for us, she'd still managed to give me the thing I wanted most. I loved her so much in that moment, I thought my heart might burst.

It wasn't until the collection bills started coming that I realized she hadn't saved for the camera at all. She'd bought it on a no-interest, no-payments-for-six-months plan. When the six months were up and she hadn't paid a dime on the thing, the creditors came calling. I finally set up a payment plan myself, taking on more babysitting and odd jobs just so the camera wouldn't get repossessed.

"I'm using the camera," I say, skirting the issue.

"You're the most talented girl I know," my mom says. "You really are."

Before I can say thanks, she's launched into her next thought.

"Honey," she says, "the washer's doing that funny thing again. That clanking? Remind me again—how do I fix it? I can't remember if I do the thing with the screwdriver or if I have to shove it."

"Right, give me a sec." I close my eyes to think, but I can't picture the machine. All I can see is my mom on the other end of the phone, wearing her scrubs and sitting in the break room of the women's clinic. Maybe she's cradling the phone in one ear while she inspects her nails. I'd bet anything she bitched about her weight to her coworkers this morning but that there's an open bag of Skittles in front of her. If she's drinking anything, I bet it's a Diet Coke. Hopefully unspiked, but who knows.

"Definitely call Henry," I say. "He'll know what to do about the washing machine." Henry is our next-door neighbor, who was a handyman back in the day. He threw out his back a year ago and pretty much sits around living off workers' comp, but if he's feeling up to it, he'll sometimes shuffle over to make free repairs for us.

"Okay. I'll call him. And I'm not sure, but I think my cell is fritzing. The screen looks all weird."

The glare of the sun is suddenly making my head hurt. "Have you tried a reboot? Where you turn everything off, then turn it on again?"

"No. Not yet."

"That's probably the best bet. If that doesn't work, you might just need to take it into the store. See if they can look at it."

"Do we have the money for that?"

"I haven't looked at the bank statements in a little while." Not since I cobbled together enough to get the water and electricity turned back on before I left, anyway.

"I just—I'm no good at this. You know that. I need my girl. You're so smart at everything. Photography. Money. Keeping your mom on track. We're a team, right?"

"We're definitely a team."

"You've been down there so long. Three weeks now! You think you'll come home soon? I just miss you so much."

"Yeah, I'm sure I'll be—" I stop. I hear loud conversations in the background on the other end of the phone. And maybe what sounds like a TV. I've seen my mom's break room. The most raucous it gets is when two women are in there at the same time, usually knitting and chatting.

"Where are you?" I ask, glancing at my watch. It's three here, same as it should be there, and it's a Thursday. So my mom should definitely be at work.

"I just walked into Larry's. Took the afternoon off."

"What happened?" I ask, praying she wasn't fired.

"Sick day. Daisy covered the desk for me."

"Mom. That's, like, a lot of sick days recently." After the accident, she must have asked me to call the clinic for her at least five times. In the few minutes it took me to make the call, then pack my bag for school, my mom had already gone back to bed and was snoring with her mouth open.

"Well, in case you didn't notice, I'm doing everything around here, Janey. I'm exhausted. I'm just trying to keep it together." I can hear her take a long swallow of something. Probably Larry's cheap house wine. I can picture the way it stains her teeth purple-gray. "Ethan's not helping my cause either. Probably he's telling you to stay down there. To leave me high and dry. Just like he did."

"Mom, no," I say. "Ethan would never say that."

"What wouldn't I say?" I spin around. Ethan's standing right behind me. I have no idea how long he's been there. Even though I know I haven't done anything wrong, I feel like I've been caught at something clandestine.

I shake my head at him and mouth "nothing."

"The van is gassed up. We need to get a move on."

Mom pipes up in my ear. "Who's that talking? Is that Ethan? Is he ready to talk to me finally? Well, give the phone over. I'll talk to him."

"No, Mom, I don't think that's wh—"

"Put him *on,* Janey."

"Wait," I say before Ethan can walk off. "It's Mom." I hold the phone out, inviting him to take it.

Ethan shakes his head. "I can't talk to her. Not now. Maybe sometime, if she gets sober. She knows that's the deal."

Anger rushes in. I hate the way he's so formulaic about it, like it's an equation. Except that Mom's not a theorem, she's a person. X + Y is the square root of Ethan's bullshit. I don't call him on it, though. Now's not the time. If Mom hears us fighting, she'll just use it as one more reason I should come home.

"He can't, Mom. Sorry."

"Are you kidding me?" Mom says. I can hear her swallow again. "Well, I hope you see this for what it is, Janey. I hope this is crystal clear. Ethan, he thinks he can do whatever he wants and just forget his own family. He's going to leave you too, you know."

"Mom, don't."

"He hates us."

"No. He just wants you to stop drinking is all."

"So I have to be perfect before we can have a relationship?"

I don't know about perfect. Maybe just better. And is that such a bad thing?

"No, but we both think you drink too much."

My mom exhales. "I went to rehab, in case you don't remember."

"I remember, but you still dr—"

"I've got this under control. Come on, how bad are things really? You think you have it tough or something? You want me to tell you how it was growing up on the Iron Range?"

She's talking about the flat, scrubby part of Minnesota where she and Uncle Pete were raised dirt-poor. I know where this is headed. She'll say that we don't really have any problems. That she had it so much worse when she was growing up, when her dad would leave for days on end, and they literally had no food, and she and Uncle Pete would go down to the stream and drink the water just so their bellies would feel full. That *I'm* the one with the issues.

Ethan steps close and puts his hands on my shoulders. "The

van's ready when you are," he says, and walks away. I watch him go, thinking about how huge the space between us seems, even though it's just from here to the van.

"Janey? Are you ignoring me?"

"No. The team just needs to hit the road."

"Sure. Leaving *again*. How convenient for you."

Something in me cracks. I can feel the fissures spreading on my skin, through my muscles, all the way into the veins in my eyes. "Don't do this, Mom."

"Excuse me? Don't do what? I'm not the one who left home. So don't act like this is my fault."

I swear I'm going to break into a thousand pieces. And then no one will ever be able to separate me from all this coffee-colored dust, and I'll be trapped in Kansas forever. Part of the dirt.

"I just want things to be okay," I whisper.

"What, they're not? What the hell is so bad about your life, Janey? Huh? Me? Am I ruining everything for you? Somehow I have these magical powers that enable me to screw up your life from way up here in Minnesota, eh?"

"Mom, no. It's not that. But don't you think . . . couldn't things be . . . better?"

The phone is quiet on the other end, save for the sound of Larry's in the background. "Mom?" I ask. "Did you hear what I said? Are you there?"

The only response is hard silence as she hangs up.

7

I stare out the van window, replaying the conversation with my mom again and again in my head. The loop is making my head ring. The part that tolls the loudest isn't about Mom. It's about Ethan. His math-professor approach to our family drives me nuts, but there's a secret part of me that envies it too. His ability to just cut ties and take off—what would that be like? I wonder.

I knock my head softly against the van's window, trying to stem the tide of thoughts. How can I sit here and think about leaving Mom the same way Ethan left us? I know firsthand how awful it feels.

And yet.

A dull ache spreads through me. Realization makes my stomach churn. I can fly my righteous flag all I want, and piss and moan about how coldly Ethan handles things, but when it comes down to it, I'm not in Minnesota either. I'm in Tornado Alley.

I'm not just thinking about leaving. I'm *gone*.

Just like him.

The question remains: for how long?

I tamp down my nausea and try to focus on the here and now. *Step on the cockroaches you can see, and worry about the infestation later,* as my mom would say. I concentrate on the other side of the van's glass, where golden wheat fields roll into a jewel-blue sky. I stare at patches of trees reflecting the early evening light. We pass a sign welcoming us into Nebraska, "the good life," and I tell myself we're going to have a peaceful evening. Maybe grab dinner somewhere and call it a day.

Everything is going to be fine.

That all changes when I catch a glimpse of the radar screen that Ethan and Stephen are studying in the seats ahead of me. The colors are changing from dark red to purple, which I used to think meant the weather was getting less severe, but Stephen taught me that, no, purple actually means, in his words, "some heavy meteorological shit is going down."

Sure enough, Mason, who is seated behind me in the van, stops chewing on his third beef stick long enough to take a good look at the sky. "Anyone else think this baby's going to produce?" he asks, squinting out the window.

From the driver's seat, Hallie glances at the darkening clouds. Victor's in the passenger seat, navigating maps. "I think we'd better get off this road and go west," Hallie says.

"Next exit," Victor says, studying the grids on his lap. Out here, GPS isn't always reliable, so the team makes sure to have old-fashioned backups.

Hallie flips on the van's lights. The thickening clouds are starting to block out the sun.

At the end of the ramp, we stop. Ethan curses softly. The road is crammed with vans, most of them filled with tourists—people who pay money to weather experts to see the storms up close. The tours are often led by scientists, but they're not there to study anything or gather data. It's more like whale watching—except with deadly storms.

Hallie leans on the horn, but nothing moves. It's like rush-hour traffic out in the middle of nowhere.

"Dammit," Stephen says. "There are more of these parasites every year." The tourists are one of the few things that can make Stephen lose his cool. "There should be laws against this kind of jam-up," he grumbles.

Stephen always says it's one thing if we don't get data because we can't find the storms, but he can't stomach the fact that we might not get the information we're after because tourists are in the way.

Victor flips to another map to see if there's a different way we can get to the storm.

"Is it me, or did this supercell really blow up in the last few minutes?" Ethan asks. "You guys seeing this?"

I stare out the window at the mass of gray sky a couple miles off. Supercells are bad thunderstorms that produce tornadoes. The edges of this one are rounded and billowing out, making it look like a spaceship hovering on the ground. I half expect to see aliens jumping out of it—but I know the only thing coming from these clouds will be a twister. If we're lucky.

The wind is so strong, trees and grass on either side of the road are bent with the force of it. On our first chase, I thought all the wind must mean a tornado was close by. But Ethan told me the wind is all the warm air getting sucked into the storm and giving it energy when it meets cold air. Lots of wind is good, but it doesn't necessarily mean, for certain, that there's a tornado around.

"Get back on the highway," Victor says to Hallie. "We gotta go back the way we came, then get on a smaller road and gun it."

Stephen's head lifts. "Is the smaller road paved?" I'm relieved to hear him ask the same question that's coursing through my brain. Lots of the back roads around here are dirt, and they can get muddy and dangerous during a storm. Ethan told me about one team from Utah that slid off the road and became stranded, only to have the twister land on top of them. Two people were killed and a third was badly injured when part of a fence went straight through his leg.

"Looks to be," Victor says. "We won't take it if it's dirt."

A few minutes later, the van is barreling south, and everyone inside it, except me (and Hallie, who's driving), is trying to get more data on the storm. I'm pointing my camera out the window, watching the gray clouds pitch and roll against the coppery evening light. It's beautiful and terrifying all at once. I want to snap the shutter, but I know it's useless to try and get anything through the van's dirt-flecked glass.

Suddenly, we turn and are going west again, way farther behind the storm than I know anyone wants to be, but at least we're on a road that's not dirt and isn't crowded with tornado tourists. "The storm's course is steady, but it *is* speeding up," Stephen says. "We need to punch it."

Victor looks at Hallie. "That means pedal to the metal," he says. From where I'm sitting, his profile reminds me of Abraham Lincoln—huge forehead, long nose.

Hallie glares at him. "Let me drive, Vic. I know what I'm doing."

I think back to the hint Stephen dropped this morning, that Victor is being a dick because something happened to him. But what? As I stare at the storm, I think I see a telltale shape. "Is that—?"

"She's dropping a funnel!" Mason yells. He's got his binoculars out, pressing them against his face, and now we're all trying to focus on what's coming out of the clouds. From this distance, it looks like the leg of a praying mantis—thin and jutting.

As we speed along, the leg thickens and loses its awkward bend. The mass darkens against the orange sky. "God, that's something," Mason breathes.

"I just wish we were closer," Ethan says. "We need to turn back north at some point. When's that going to happen, Victor?"

Victor's gaze snaps back and forth from the road to the map. "Shit!" he cries. "Hallie, go now!" Hallie hesitates for only a fraction of an instant. Then she slams on the brakes. I'm thrown forward so hard, my shoulder hits the seat in front of me. I hear Stephen grunt and Mason swear.

"The hell?" Ethan asks as the van swerves and we're suddenly going north on a road that cropped up out of nowhere. I right myself in the seat and blink. My shoulder burns from the impact. "What was that?"

"I'm sorry," Hallie says. "God, you guys, I'm so—"

"You want to get to this storm or not?" Victor interrupts.

"Not at the expense of people's safety, I don't," Stephen says. He hands Ethan his laptop, which had been thrown onto the floor of the van.

"So I'm putting people in danger again?" Victor asks. "Are you worried people are going to get hurt because I'm a constant fuckup? Is that it?"

Stephen opens his mouth like he's going to argue, then thinks better of it and simply goes back to the radar. From my seat I can see Hallie's white-knuckled grip on the steering wheel.

"Oh, no," Ethan says suddenly. He makes me worry that maybe we're too close to the storm.

"*Now* what?" I ask.

"Patchy Falls."

"What the hell is Patchy Falls?" Mason asks.

I can see Ethan swallow, can see the way his muscles tighten. I feel mine do the same.

"Patchy Falls is a *town*," Ethan says. "And the tornado's right on top of it."

8

The world has gone dark, but the sinking sun has backlit the tornado, making our view of it literally rosy. Hallie parks the van on a small rise, and we all bolt out of the doors. The arctic air is biting.

"Holy cold front, Batman!" Mason yells above the wind. He and Victor race to the back of the van to begin unloading the chasing equipment—most importantly, Polly.

Victor kneels next to her, flipping switches and calibrating her devices. "What's that new display?" Mason asks, pointing at a small screen.

"She's got self-monitoring capabilities now," Victor replies. "Gets too wet, too hot, she shuts down. I think she flaked on that last chase because of the high humidity."

Mason punches the air. "Holy shit you're a genius!" I zoom in on him to snap a few photos, capturing Mason's open-mouthed glee. Then I move the lens to Victor. He's stoic in the wind and noise, but I notice his hands are shaking. I wonder if every chaser gets so excited about storms, they tremble.

Polly is barely up and running when Hallie points at the sky. "Look!"

I train my lens on the distance. What look like splinters are swirling in the filmy air around the twister, except they're probably tree trunks or limbs. Bursts of energy from exploding power transformers—or maybe it's lightning—flare white-hot against the dark sky every few seconds. The wind is so loud, I can hardly hear my own thoughts.

"I hope no one's hurt!" I yell, then instantly regret opening my mouth. Once again, it's filled with the dust and sand particles getting whipped up by the wind. I spit a few times into the dirt, trying not to gag.

When my tongue is finally clear of grit, I snap pictures of Patchy Falls' water tower and a short row of houses. The tornado spins behind them. I hit the shutter again and again, praying everyone in Patchy Falls has found a basement.

I watch as the twister's color starts to change from coal to a light blue.

"It's roping out," Stephen says, his eyes on the churning sky. "She's not going to last much longer."

I know this sucks for Polly's readings, but I'm glad for Patchy Falls' sake that the storm was on the ground for only a few minutes.

Ethan's got his hands on his hips, watching the tornado weaken. The howl all around us starts to quiet. "Did we get *any* solid data?" he asks.

Mason's studying Polly, his hair a shade darker thanks to all the dirt and dust that's now in it. I can only imagine what my own looks like. "I'm not sure. Where did Victor go? He should probably look her over."

"I'm right here," Victor says, walking up. He squats in the grass next to Polly. "If there are numbers there, I'll get them. I can analyze everything tonight, once we find a motel."

"Not before we check out Patchy Falls," Stephen says. "We need to see if anyone in that town needs help."

"Oh, come on," Victor says. "The tornado wasn't on the ground that long. Everybody's probably fine."

"Lightning and winds still could have done damage," Stephen replies.

Victor rolls his eyes, but doesn't argue further. Which is a good thing because helping people is the point of what *any* chaser does. Whatever data the Torbros or the Blisters or the other teams get will all be used toward one end: giving people more warning ahead of a storm and keeping them safe.

Right now, though, the science is still a ways off. And here, real people in a real town have been hit by a bona fide storm, and some of them could be hurt—or even dead.

"Let's get this over with, then," Victor says, and I'm suddenly aware of how clean he is. His Torbros T-shirt is free of dirt. There aren't any flecks of mud or sand in his hair, like there are on the rest of us. Even his fingernails look clean.

"Where did you go?" I ask him. "Were you in the van when the twister touched down?" I figure that's the only way he could have stayed this impeccable.

Victor turns his dark eyes on me. "I'm sorry. I didn't realize we were all reporting to you now. Got a minute to sign my time sheet?"

"Hey," says Ethan. "Watch it."

Victor points a finger at him. "Then tell your sister to back off. Someone needs to be watching the radar. Okay? Plain and simple."

Except nobody watches the radar when the storm is right there. That's like watching an event on TV when it's happening live, right in front of you. Not that I'm about to say that, though. Victor stomps back to the van, and I pretend to check something on my camera until Polly's loaded and we can go.

Hallie eases alongside me. "Don't take the Victor stuff too hard," she says. Her cheekbones are speckled with dirt, her blond hair knotted and wild. "It's not you. Everyone knows that it's him."

"What's his deal?" I ask. "Has he always been this much of a jerk?"

"He's always had sort of an attitude, but not like this."

"What happened?" I ask, thinking back to the conversation at breakfast.

Hallie glances around, then pulls me off to the side. "Last season, we punched the core of this storm—"

"You what?"

"Punching the core is when you drive through the heavy precipitation and hail to get to the twister. Chasers as a rule try to avoid that because it's super dangerous. But in this case, we were desperate for some data. So we went through the core."

"What happened?"

"First, we got pelted with crazy hail. It cracked the windshield over and over. And then the rain was so heavy, we couldn't see the twister. It was a bad chase, and getting worse. Stephen wanted to turn around and just call everything off, but Victor kept pushing him. So we kept going and then suddenly Ethan yelled, and I was driving, so I slammed on the brakes. Next thing I know, it's like this whipped-up fog is in front of us, only it's not fog but the twister. The whole van starts to shake, and Victor's window blows out. Just like that."

I swallow, thinking about the glass shattering on Cat and me during the accident.

"I threw it into reverse and tried to get us out of there. I floored it, but there was this suction—the updraft. The van was hardly moving, just a few miles an hour. I thought we were going to die, one hundred percent. The whole van was rocking, side to side. And then, Stephen screams at me to turn the wheel so I'm backing up at an angle. Something about the wind shear. I don't know, but he was screaming, and what else could I do? So I just did it. The van broke free of the wind, and the tires started peeling. But right as we gained traction, this twisted piece of metal came through Victor's broken window."

Hallie glances at the ground, then at me. "There was nothing to stop it, and it hit Victor in the face. There was blood everywhere. It splattered the window and was on the seat. All over *me*. Victor made this noise, kind of like a sheep, actually. As weird as that sounds. It was this noise that sounded like 'baaaa,' but it was so much worse. I thought—I thought he'd *died*. I screamed and reversed us the hell out of there. We made it, but Victor . . ."

The realization hits me. "His scar?"

Hallie nods. "He was in the hospital for almost a week. He had to have so many stitches, and they spent hours trying to get all the metal out. The doctors said a few more millimeters, and most of the metal would have gone into his frontal lobe."

"Oh."

"The weird thing was, he wasn't that upset about his wound. At least not at first. It was more like he felt he was a failure and he put us in danger. I think because of that, he was desperate to get back out in the field, to prove everything was okay. So, about a month later, at the very end of the season, he started chasing again. His first time back out, the setup was perfect. We were tracking a storm that had been building all day, and just about every chase team was on it. It was textbook, totally classic. But when it started to produce, Victor freaked. We were on this back road with at least ten other teams and suddenly Victor starts screaming. He's blubbering and yelling and cowering with his hands over his head. It was so sad. And of course every other chaser *around* got to witness it.

"And now, this season, Victor might not be cowering, but he definitely acts like he's still scared of storms or something. Scared to take risks, to get close. Only because he's Victor, he can't say that. So he just walks around acting like a tool."

"Oh," I say again.

"It's nuts," Hallie says, picking at the dirt around her fingernail. "But the worst part is, people like Alex Atkins are being such jerks. Like with that bet? Alex added the last part about the teams staying intact because he thinks Victor is going to quit. Stop chasing and walk away."

"Will he?" I ask.

"Stephen doesn't think so. He says it's just a phase. Which is good for us because Victor might be an asshole, but he's still a good scientist. And he's a whiz with Polly."

"Yo!" Ethan calls out. He motions with his hand. "Gear's in. Let's go."

"In general, we don't talk about it a lot," Hallie says as we trot to the van. "Hang out with any other chase team and you'll probably hear Victor's story within ten minutes. But I think we all just keep hoping he'll change. That he'll go back to being the way he was."

Hope is the blindfold stupid people use so they don't have to see the truth, my mom would say. I can't help but think that in this case, she might be a little right. Victor doesn't seem like he's snapping out of this any time soon.

"I hope so," I say to Hallie, because even if the odds are against it, Victor not being so much of a dick *would* be nice for the whole team.

I pull the door shut behind me, and Hallie starts the engine. We're all silent as the van covers the short distance to Patchy Falls.

9

We pass a sign that says PATCHY FALLS: WE'RE UP TO GREAT THINGS! then inch along Main Street. Leaves plaster the wet sidewalks in damp clumps, and I spot a couple blown-out windows, but everything seems mostly okay. A few people are walking around studying the street, then the sky, then the street again. Hallie slows and lowers her window. "You guys need some help?" she asks a bearded man and what looks like his son. "Anybody hurt?"

The man shakes his head, pulls his son closer. They seem like they've just rolled out of bed—hair tousled, expressions confused. I figure it's the shock of the storm. "Most folks this block are fine," the man replies. "I hear some trees went down over near Jersey Street. That's where we're headed."

"Straight ahead?" Hallie asks, pointing. The man nods. Hallie raises the window, and we keep going.

"Wires," Victor says, and Hallie brakes. I crane my neck and see twisted black lines snaking across the street. "We either walk it or back up and try to find another way in."

"I vote walk," Ethan says. He opens the van door, and we hear police sirens. Other than that, it's eerily still.

"Walk it is," Stephen says. "Careful of lines and debris, people. Don't get too close to anything that looks remotely unstable."

We pick our way through the streets and keep mostly quiet. I'm grateful for my camera, so I have something to do besides just look at this stuff. I mean, I *am* looking—but the camera makes me feel safer. Like at least there's something between me and the destruction.

Sometimes I think it's easier for me to see things, period, if I have the camera in my hand. It's borderline magical to me, the way a camera can take something that's ugly—a pile of bills on the counter, say—and just by adjusting the tilt, the zoom, turn it into something beautiful. Once, while she slept, I took a picture of my mom's lips, dry and cracking from dehydration, her breath sour as it escaped from behind them. The two bleached tombstones of her front teeth were barely visible. In the morning light, the black-and-white photo I snapped came out looking like—I don't know, the desert or something. Rugged and chapped and wild. It should have been gross, but I stared at it for hours. It was gorgeous.

We pass a church with half the roof gone and stained glass sprinkled on the grass like confetti. "Okay," Stephen says, "it's going to start to get dark in a few minutes. Let's put together a plan."

"We have to keep canvassing," Ethan says. "We have to make sure no one's hurt." The rest of the team agrees, and moments later we've split up, each of us armed with walkie-talkies and flashlights, searching for anyone who needs help.

I walk south, away from Jersey Street. I don't have to go far before the homes thin out. The hulking shadows around me are mostly pole barns and garages. I cross a set of railroad tracks, picking my way past twisted metal, a couple cars, and the splinters of wrecked street signs.

"Hello!" I yell. "Does anyone need help?"

The only sound is an empty plastic cup tumbling across the road.

Lightning flashes in the sky, and the wind picks up again. I zip my jacket and decide I'll go just a little farther, when I'm stopped in my tracks by a voice.

"Hello?" I yell, wondering if I've imagined it. I shine my flashlight beam into the darkness, splitting apart the night. But I don't see anything.

I stand perfectly still, straining to hear. There it is again—a high wail that sounds like it's all vowels. *Aaaoouuueeaii*. Someone's calling out. I race back across the railroad tracks, sprinting toward the sound. I round a corner closer to Jersey Street, then stop. There's a van on its side.

"Hello?" I slow my steps. The next thing I know, someone's climbing out of the van's shattered passenger window.

My flashlight beam lands on the face of a woman, maybe around thirty, with clumps of dirt matted into her brown hair.

"Help," she croaks. She's trying to pull herself out of the small space.

"Don't move!" I cry, rushing forward. I click on the walkie-talkie. "This is Jane. I'm south of Jersey Street, and I need help! Does anyone copy?"

The only answer is static.

And in the distance, the rumbling thunder warns of another storm rolling in.

10

This is bad. My heart pounds and my hands shake, but I force myself to breathe, to stay calm, to treat it like it's my mom and I need to get her to bed or to work. "Stay still," I say to the woman, crouching down. The van's on its side, and this lady is about halfway through the passenger window, on her knees. The way the car is positioned, it's almost like she's popping out of a hatch. "Are you hurt anywhere?"

"My right ankle," she says, her eyes wild and unfocused. She's probably in shock, but she's at least lucid. "I think it twisted when the van rolled."

"Okay," I say. "We need to get you out of there, which I'm betting we can if you turn sideways and I pull. If you keep your weight on your left side, I think your ankle should be okay."

She nods and shimmies sideways, so her body fits better in the window. I put my hands under her arms. "Count of three, you wiggle and I pull, okay?" She nods.

"One, two—three!"

Her body comes free in a matter of seconds. She puts her weight on me to climb clear of the door and, as she does, I notice her right arm has a deep gash on it. I wish I had a first-aid kit or at least a bandage, but they're all back with the Torbros.

"Can you lean on me and make it over to that downed tree?" I ask, motioning to a massive trunk a few feet away. She nods, and we stumble-limp to where she can sit.

I ask her if she can tell me her name.

"Danielle." A pause. "Danny. Danny Bowstrom."

I think back to my first-aid training in health class freshman year. "Do you know what month it is?"

"July."

I breathe a little easier. If she can answer questions right, it means that she probably doesn't have a head injury on top of everything else. Still, when I roll up the leg of her pants, her ankle's swollen to the point where I know she needs a doctor.

Once again, I try the walkie-talkie to radio Ethan and the rest of the team.

"This is Jane. Is anyone there?" Nothing happens. I pull out my cell phone and try dialing Ethan, but I can't get a signal. All the towers around us are down.

Lightning flashes, and I wonder if a supercell is going to land on top of us at any second. Worry churns my stomach, but I force myself to smile at Danny. "No problem," I say. "We'll find someone." There's help four blocks up toward Jersey Street—the question is whether I should try to walk there with Danny or wait for help to come to us. I'm not sure how much time there is before the sky might explode.

I try the walkie again. "Hello," I say. "Come in, please." I stop when my voice cracks on *please*. I don't want Danny to know I'm starting to panic.

I cup my hands and yell with every ounce of lung power I have. "Help! Someone, please!"

I inhale and am ready to bellow again when all the air whooshes out of me.

With lightning crackling in the sky behind him, Max is jogging toward me.

I'm so relieved, I almost hug him. I stop myself, though, before my arms can wrap themselves around his neck. I notice he has a first-aid kit.

"Jane." He puts a hand on my shoulder, lets it slide down my arm. Max's eyes rake my body. I'm almost shocked, until I realize he thinks *I'm* the one who's hurt. "Tell me what's wrong." His green eyes find mine, and my heart flutters at the concern there.

"No, not me. Her." I jerk my chin toward where Danny is sitting. She's slumped, head in her hands.

Before he can turn to help her, I grab his hand. "Do you have a walkie? I can't reach anyone." I'm trying not to notice the heat of his skin against mine.

"I don't," he says. "But we'll get help. Don't worry."

I nod, and Max kneels next to Danny. I see the strength in his arms, in his shoulders. Thunder rumbles, and I blink. What is my problem? I'm losing it over a boy I've barely said ten words to, when this is no time to get butterflies. We've got to move before the next storm is on us.

I try both my phone and the walkie over and over while Max cleans the wound on Danny's arm and puts a bandage on it. I still can't get through to anyone, but at least Danny seems to be hanging in there.

A cold drizzle starts, and I look to Danny's van, wondering for an insane second if we could stand it up and drive away. That's before my flashlight beam catches the crunched grill and at least one missing tire. Even if we could get it righted, there's no way we could drive it. I'm about ready to click my flashlight off when I spot the words "Danny's Lookout Van" painted crudely on the side.

"Are you a spotter?" I ask, wondering if she's one of those people who volunteers to watch the skies. No matter how good radar is, it's no substitute for actual field observations, and professional weather teams, like the Torbros, can't be everywhere at once.

"I got certified as a spotter by the county this spring," Danny says, "and I went out to follow this storm today. Make sure I could radio in a funnel cloud to the county if I saw one, and we could get those sirens going to warn people. I thought I knew what it was doing. Then it started raining, and I got turned around. Next thing I know, I'm right under the twister. I don't remember much, just all this sound and shaking, then I was upside down."

"You're lucky to be alive," Max says. It could be a jab, but it's not. He's just being truthful. I'd heard about spotters who'd tried to chase down tornadoes without the right equipment or experience, who wound up getting really hurt in the process.

Chasing is dangerous, period. Even the Torbros mess up—and we have Victor's scar, not to mention attitude, to show for it.

Max takes Danny's hand. "My team is back a few blocks, and they have a medic. If you can put your weight on Jane and me, we'll get you over there, and a doctor will check you out."

I glance up at the sky, hoping Danny can walk fast enough to find help before the next storm starts to really pick up—but not so fast that she reinjures herself. After we get Danny to her feet, Max looks at me and winks. "Told you we'd see each other on a chase," he says.

I smile and we start the slow trek back to the Twister Blisters. But we've only gone a few steps when we hear swearing.

"Dammit." I know the voice immediately. It's Victor. His flashlight beam finds us as a peal of thunder shakes the sky. "Jane, what are you doing? We've been looking for you for twenty minutes."

For once, I'm relieved to see him. "Thank God you're here," I say. "We're trying to get this woman help. Can you radio the other Torbros?"

Victor barely glances at Danny. "We need to get moving. Leave the kid with her and let's go."

I stare at him. "What?"

"I said, let's *move*."

My feet don't budge. "Absolutely not."

Victor might be petrified that we're going to get caught in another storm, but no *way* am I going to leave Max and Danny alone.

"This guy for real?" Max asks me.

"Unfortunately."

"You got a problem?" Victor asks Max.

"You got a *walkie*?" Max replies. "Last I checked, we had an injured person here who needs treatment. We'd love it if there was a medic waiting by the time we get to Jersey Street. Better yet, one who could help us get her there. Think you could at least make that call for help before you run away?"

"C'mon, Jane," Victor says, turning to go.

"Dammit, make the call before you run—" I stop when I spot a blinking red light a few feet off.

In the moments that follow, the only sound is crickets and wind. And a whirring from a small machine. Victor freezes, and Max curses quietly.

From out of the shadows steps a cameraman. A spotlight flips on, and my eyes squint against the white light while my heart plummets all the way to my feet.

It's the Weather Network. And they've been filming every word we've said.

11

Danny speaks first. "Turn that crap off," she says. "My head hurts, and I need a doctor—not an interview." When the cameraman flips off his spotlight and pauses filming, I want to hug Danny until her ribs crack.

"Hey, Volksie," Max says to the curly-haired cameraman. It's not one of the guys from that morning, but it would make sense that the Weather Network would have a team of cameramen, and that Max would recognize them.

"Hey," Volksie replies. With the spotlight off and the flashlights on, I see he's not much older than Max and me. He's dressed in skinny jeans and a T-shirt that says BAREFOOT DISCO!

"We, uh, could use some help," Max says. "If you have a radio, could you tell the Blisters we're on our way and we need a medic?"

Volksie nods. "Yeah. No problem." After he sends the message through, Max glances at the sky. The drizzle has tapered off, but that doesn't necessarily mean anything. We could still get hammered with high winds and hail any second.

"Danny, you think you can try and keep walking? Jane and I will support you." Danny nods and we start our slow shuffle. Volskie flips the spotlight and camera back on.

"Seriously, can you turn that shit off?" Victor asks, shielding his eyes against the glaring light. "I didn't authorize you to record me."

You would say that, I think, because you're acting like a dickwad.

Volksie isn't fazed. "You can take it up with a producer."

That's when I realize Victor is wearing the TORBROS: WE CHASE CHICKS AND STORMS shirt. If the Weather Network plays this footage of us, everybody's going to know that the guy who wanted to leave the injured woman behind, in the dark, is a Tornado Brother.

Fabulous.

Thunder crashes, and we all jump. "Screw this," Victor says, breaking into a run. Within seconds, he's disappeared into the dark. Max puts a hand on Danny's elbow. "It's not far, I promise. Let's just keep going." Danny nods, and we soldier on. With the camera rolling, we pick our way through the debris and back to our teams.

By the time we get to Jersey Street, it's a circus. Cop cars are parked here and there, their lights flashing blue and red against the nearby homes. They've set up floodlights and searchlights so rescuers can see what they're doing.

Handfuls of people are standing around, watching. Others are checking for broken gas mains, or making sure anyone who needs help gets it. News vans have already showed up to report on the situation.

An EMT rushes forward and helps us get Danny onto a stretcher. Max follows them to a waiting ambulance, while I squint through the crowd to try and get my bearings. I spot the Twisters easily, because they're the ones with more Weather Network cameras on them. Fortunately, the Torbros are nearby too.

Relief floods Ethan's face when he spots me. "Jane!" He clears an overturned tree to get to me. I close my eyes and fight off the sudden urge to bawl, thinking how nice it is to have this reaction from him. I wait for his hug, but I open my eyes a moment later when I don't feel anything.

Ethan is staring at me, arms stiff at his sides. "We couldn't reach you," he says. "We sent Victor out for you, but then he didn't come back either. We didn't know what had *happened*." His eyes are more scared than mad.

"My walkie broke. And someone was hurt."

"But I didn't know that. Jesus, I was so *worried*." His hands are actually shaking.

"Ethan, it's okay—"

"It's not okay! This can't ever happen again. Understand?"

His raised voice makes my skin crawl. I nod, but part of me wants to get up in his face. Because it's not like I was *trying* to lose contact with him. That was purely an accident. What's more, Ethan can't go missing for five years and then suddenly decide to play Parent of the Year. It doesn't work like that.

Except now's not the time to fight. The cameras are on us and, besides, there might be another storm on the way.

"Do we need to get all these people to safety?" I ask, glancing around. "Is there another storm rolling in?"

"It looked bad for a bit," Ethan says, taking a breath, "but it's breaking up and going north."

That's one bit of good news at least.

"You going to tell me what happened out there?"

"We found this woman Danny," I say. "She needed help, so I stopped for her. I wasn't about to leave her there."

I don't mention the part where Victor abandoned her, hurt and untreated.

"She's over there," I add, pointing to the ambulance. "She's a spotter, and during the storm she got turned around and ended up right underneath the twister."

Ethan rubs his eyes for a moment. "Then that's two people hurt in Patchy Falls," he says. "The police said the pastor of that church we saw went to the hospital for some minor injuries and then there's Danny here."

I let Ethan take the conversation in a different direction. "So no deaths," I say.

Ethan nods. "No deaths. Jersey Street has a lot of trees and wires down, but the houses are mostly in good shape. They got lucky."

"They got *really* lucky," Stephen says, approaching us.

Another Weather Network light snaps on, and suddenly I can see all the dirt and dust from the earlier chase in Stephen's beard and Ethan's hair. I wonder if we'll all make our first appearances on national television looking like refugees.

"EF-2 you think?" Ethan asks. He's back in weather mode, one hundred percent.

Stephen nods. "Yeah, EF-2."

EF stands for Enhanced Fujita, and is a scale that measures a twister's size based on factors like wind speed and damages. The scale goes from zero to five.

"Definitely would have been an EF-3 if it had stayed on the ground much longer," Ethan says. "Everyone's fortunate it wasn't worse than it was."

"I wouldn't use the word *fortunate* if I were you," says a voice. It's Alex Atkins, now standing with us. Somehow his pants and Twister Blisters polo look fresh and pressed. Every one of the hairs on his head is perfectly in place. "From what I can tell, you guys were pretty far behind the storm. We were closer, so I guess we count this tornado as ours."

Stephen's expression doesn't change. "Not sure this is the best time to be talking about the bet, Alex," he says. "Our focus should be Patchy Falls. Don't you think?"

Alex just laughs. "Oh, that's rich, coming from the Torbros."

"Excuse me?"

"Come on, don't act like you don't know."

"Don't know what, exactly?" Stephen asks.

Alex looks around, like he's searching for people to agree with him. "Just heard from our cameraman Volksie that your brother was walking through Patchy Falls ignoring storm victims. That lady over there," he hitches his thumb toward Danny, "was bleeding in an overturned van, and he wouldn't help. Ask your little intern here." He looks at me. "She saw the whole thing."

Stephen locks his gaze on mine. "Is this true?"

I know Ethan is staring at me with the same intensity as Stephen. I know he's thinking I should have told him all this right off the bat. But the cameras were still rolling, and Ethan was acting like a tool. I look at the wet blacktop. "Yes."

Stephen clears his throat. "I'm sorry to hear that. This isn't how anyone in the chasing community should conduct themselves." He pauses. "I think the Torbros need to have a meeting immediately. Ethan, help me round up Victor. Jane, please head back to the van."

I nod, glad to have somewhere to go, a direction to get me away from the cameras. Before I take two steps, Stephen presses a functioning walkie into my hand. "Just in case," he says. "The van's about twenty yards off to your left. Mason and Hallie are already there. Join up with them, and we'll see you in a few minutes." His deep voice is soothing. It's like he's telling me not to worry, which is more than I can say for Ethan, who I wish hadn't gone all Lifetime movie on me and acted like I'd *tried* to stir up drama.

I count my steps to clear my head. Thirty-one, thirty-two . . . By the next block, darkness engulfs me, and I stop counting. The clouds overhead thin for a moment, and I see a patch of stars. Then I feel a hand on my elbow and jump.

"We have to stop meeting like this," Max says.

12

Max keeps his hand on my elbow, and I don't ask him to move it. The air is thick with the smell of grass and splintered wood. There are no floodlights or police cars on this street. A few shapes and flashlight beams move here and there, but for the most part, Max and I are wrapped in darkness.

"I have an idea," he says.

"I have two," I reply, thinking I'd like to put my hand in his hand, my lips on his lips. In the space of one twister, my mind's gone from being blank around Max to a kaleidoscope of thoughts vivid enough to make me blush.

"Mine first," Max says. I tune in when I hear the urgency in his voice. "That footage of Victor is a total cluster. Makes your team look awful. I heard one of the camera guys say it could really bite you in the ass if they show it. Loss of funding maybe."

I nod. I'm guessing Stephen thinks the same thing, which is why he's calling an emergency meeting.

"But I heard something else, too. Alex was asking the Weather Network if they'd want footage of the Blisters sticking around Patchy Falls to help clean the place up. The network guys were practically jizzing in their pants they were so excited about it."

"Okay," I say slowly, trying to follow Max's logic. "And all this affects me because?"

"Because of my idea."

"Why do I have this sudden feeling I should be worried?"

"Because maybe you should."

Every hair on my arms is standing on end. I suppose the way Max takes charge, takes what he wants out of every situation he's in, should piss me off. But instead, it's making my body feel like it's hooked up to a generator.

"Let's hear this idea."

"I think your team should stay and help clean up Patchy Falls, too. Weather Network cameras will be here filming the Blisters anyway, and there's no way they won't put the Torbros on camera if they're around too. I mean, come on. Two rival teams helping clean up a town? It's so money. *And* you can put Victor front and center doing good deeds that show he's not an asshole. They film that and air it, you guys don't look so bad."

"Clean up the town?" I ask. "Like, we get hammers and nails and help them rebuild or something?"

"Or just help them get those downed branches into Dumpsters. Or get them hot meals. Whatever they need."

"And who, exactly, convinces the Torbros this is a good idea?"

"You do."

I stop walking. Somewhere in the distance, a police siren wails, then fades. "You found me in the dark to tell me I should convince my team to stop chasing and clean up a town? Sorry if I sound a little skeptical here, but you *are* a Twister Blister. How do I know this isn't a setup so you guys have a better shot at winning the bet? How do I know the Twister Blister trucks won't be gone in the morning?"

Max steps closer to me. We're not touching, but I swear I can still feel him. "It's not a setup."

"Then why?"

Max steps back. He clicks on his flashlight so we can actually see each other's faces.

"Maybe I think you're cool, and I want to see more of you. I'd rather not wait for the next twister—whenever that might be. I'd rather make it so running into you happens less by chance and more by design."

I've never had a guy tell me he thinks I'm cool and wants to see more of me. Ever.

"Yeah?" I ask.

Max laughs. "*Yeah.* I wouldn't make that up."

I hear voices and see bouncing pinpoints of light approaching. Max grabs my hands. "Look, whatever happens, just know—I'm not bullshitting you. And I mean what I say about wanting to spend more time with you. If it doesn't happen in Patchy Falls, that's cool. Maybe we can make it happen some other time."

I nod, even though *some other time* sounds far away and

impractical. Max squeezes my hands, and fireworks go off in my brain.

"All right," I agree. "I'll talk to the Torbros."

Max releases me, and I want to touch the place where his fingers were, but I don't. "See you soon, I hope," he says, and disappears into the night.

Victor is the last one into the van, probably because he knows Stephen is furious with him. The air inside the vehicle is close and heavy. The dim dome light barely cuts the darkness. Hallie moves to start the engine, but Stephen stops her. "Not yet," he says. "We have some things to discuss."

In the following seconds, no one asks him what's up. We all know what Victor did. We all know this could be the end of the Torbros' funding.

"I want to remind everyone," Stephen begins, "that our mission—the reason we're out here in the first place—is to help people. And the minute we stop doing that, we have failed on *every* level."

"Look," Victor says, turning around in the front passenger seat, "that lady didn't seem that hurt. I wasn't trying to—"

"Quiet," Stephen says, cutting him off. "This isn't just about you. This is about the team. And if we lose our funding because of your issues, then *everyone's* got to regroup. And I just want to remind everyone that whether you chase with the Torbros or someone else, the point of everything we do is to help people. At every turn. Got it?"

The whole van mumbles yes. Except Victor. "Lose funding?

What are you talking about, Steve? That lady is fine. Just a scratch."

"It wasn't just a scratch," Stephen says. "She needed medical attention." His eyes flash with anger and, for a second, Victor looks crushed by the hardness there, but he regroups quickly.

"Well, I didn't give the Weather Network permission to record me. It's not like they can just put my face on TV. I still don't understand how this is such a big deal."

"Your shirt, dumbass," Mason says from the backseat. "Even if they pixel out your face, you're clearly a Torbro."

Victor looks down. His face pales as the realization sets in. "Well, it's . . . it's hardly a . . . what I did wasn't that bad," he stumbles.

"Yes, it was," I say. "You said on camera that we should leave someone who was hurt. And then you ran away and left us."

Victor glares at me. "I was only there in the first place because of *you*. I had to go back and make sure you had a babysitter."

"Don't blame me for this," I snap.

"Jesus, what are you even *doing* here?" Victor says. "Can we all just admit we don't need all those fucking pictures on the site? I mean, whatever mommy issues you and Ethan have to work out, I think maybe it's time you work them out somewhere else."

"Back off, Victor," Ethan interrupts. "You're the one screwing up here, not Jane."

"Oh, sure," Victor retorts, "says the guy who couldn't wait to put Polly up for collateral in that bet, on the off chance he could get his face on television. You had no right putting my invention up there like that. We lose her this season, it's your fault."

"You could have said something about it at the time if you'd been there. But you weren't. You'd run off. *Again*."

"Whatever," Victor says. "You're just mad because we're in a van that says Tornado *Brothers* on the side. And last time I checked, you weren't a brother."

"Oh, right, because you being Stephen's older brother has helped us out *so* much," Ethan says.

"Hey!" Stephen shouts. "That's enough. We don't need to tear ourselves apart here. We're a team. All of us are Torbros. Everyone. Period. End of story. Got it?"

My hands tremble, even as I nod. I hate Victor. I want him to get what he deserves. I want thousands of people to watch the Weather Network and hear him tell me to leave Danny. But I can't *not* pitch Max's plan just because Victor's a selfish jerk. All the rest of the Torbros could lose big if we don't do *something*.

"Listen," I say after a moment, "there could be a way to fix this. Maybe."

As clearly as I can, I outline the plan that Max came up with: that we hole up here, cleaning Patchy Falls with the Twister Blisters. The Weather Network crews can get footage of Victor and the whole team doing more good than bad. And that might be the PR we need to keep our funding.

"How do you even know that's going to work?" Victor says when I'm done.

"I don't," I reply. "But it's not like *you're* coming up with any plans."

Ethan studies me. "It's not a bad idea *if* the Twister Blisters are going to stick around. Without them, the Weather Network cameras go too. But do we know if the Blisters are staying put or taking off?"

"We don't, not for sure," I say, "but I heard a Blister talking about it." I can't very well tell them I'm going on the word of a boy I met at breakfast that day.

"But what if other storms crop up?" Mason asks from the backseat. "Aren't we supposed to have Polly out in the field? Aren't we supposed to be chasing?"

"The forecast for this week looks fairly calm," Stephen says. "It could all change, of course, but we might not be missing out on that much."

"It's a good plan," Hallie says, her fingers tapping the steering wheel. "We should at least try it." I give her a small smile, grateful for the support.

"All right," Stephen says finally. "Maybe I can find Alex tonight, talk to him, and try to suss out what his team's going to do. They're staying in Clarkstown, a few miles over. Let's head that way too. I hear they have a couple hotels and the power's not out."

Hallie starts the engine and flicks on the headlights. The beams illuminate scattered branches and torn trees. We pull onto the main road and speed away from Patchy Falls—for now, anyway.

13

Two hours later, I'm lying like a starfish on the polyester motel bedspread and staring at my cell. Three missed calls, three voice mails, all from my mom.

I push Play and listen. They start out fine. "Hey, Janey. Call me, okay? I'm sorry I hung up on you. I'm mad at Ethan, not you. I love you."

I delete it and hit Next. "Heeey, Janey." Larry's is louder in the background now. It must be filled with people by this time. I can practically see the cracked leather on the old seats at the bar and the bright neon Pabst sign that makes everyone's skin look blue. "I forgot to tell you about my friend Rodger. He's right here. Say hi, Rodger." The phone sounds like it's dunked underwater, then my mom comes back on. "Rodger is soooo nice. He sells"—she giggles—"he sells *ball bearings*. You'd like him."

I can picture Rodger just fine. Early fifties, cheap shirt, too much booze in him. The next in a long line of guys my mom is too good for.

"Oh, that reminds me," she continues, "that man you like is coming to Minneapolis. To one of the museums. Adam. Aaaaddamm . . ." She trails off, trying to remember. The phone snuffles again. "Oh, yah, Larry. I'll have another. Thanks. Okay, well, good talking to you, Janey. Right, it's Ansel Adams. His stuff is—well, I think it's on a wall somewhere. In Minneapolis. Okay? I love you."

I close my eyes. Mom wants to take me to an Ansel Adams exhibit. I haven't been to one of the Minneapolis museums since fifth grade when we went on an all-day field trip. My stomach should be fluttering, thinking about the way the sharp prints hang perfectly against white walls or the way people's heels click as they file by, taking in images of Yosemite. Joshua Tree. Mexico.

Except the thought of it just makes me tired.

Because it won't happen the way you want it to. Cat's words find me, even in my daydream. I can already hear her asking if my mom will be drunk when we go. And if so, will I let her drive? It doesn't even take Cat's voice to point out the next truth. That there's an even better chance that, when I get back to Minnesota, my mom will pretend like she never suggested the Adams exhibit at all.

But the *hope* of it happening is so real, I can almost fold my fingers around it. It *could* happen. And it *could* be crazy and fun and hilarious—all those things my mom can be when she's not sitting on a barstool at Larry's or wetting her own bed.

But how much more tired will I get waiting around for *could*?

I press Play on the third message. "Heeeeey, Janey." Larry's is still pounding in the background. "Yoouu knoow, I just—"

I can't take it. I hit Delete and shove the phone back in my pocket. *Enough.*

I stand up and smooth out the bedspread. I fluff the battered pillows and straighten the early-model alarm clock on the bedside table. It reads 11:34. I'm not tired, and there's a twenty-four-hour diner next door. My stomach rumbles, since we chased straight through dinner. Maybe some eggs and a cup of coffee will make me feel better. I grab my sweatshirt and room key and head for Happy's.

The parking lot of Happy's is all but deserted, save for a single truck and an old beater that looks more like a boat than a car. The warm lights from inside reflect on the still-wet concrete in panels of gold.

Inside, booths with fat, red plastic seats line one wall. On the other side of the checkered floor is a counter flanked by stainless-steel stools. On one of the stools sits Ethan. His head pops up when I enter. "Look what the supercell dragged in," he jokes, patting the seat next to him. I hop up and swivel so I'm facing him.

"Fancy meeting you here," I say.

"Of all the diners in all the towns in all of Tornado Alley," he says in an awful *Casablanca* impression, "she walks into mine." He smiles, but his eyes are tired and bloodshot. A five-o'clock shadow darkens his jaw. I wonder if he's thinking about Patchy Falls . . . or something else entirely.

"So just you tonight?" I ask. "No chasing entourage?"

"Nope. Just me. And my thoughts, which are few and far between, so it's good to have your company."

A round waitress with dark hair and friendly hazel eyes parks herself in front of me. "What can I get you, sweetie?" she asks.

I glance over the menu. "French toast," I say, scrapping the idea of eggs. "And a cup of coffee, please."

The waitress glances at Ethan's half-eaten pie. It looks like lemon meringue. "You still working?"

Ethan nods. "Still working."

She puts a hand on one ample hip. "The apple's better. Didn't I say the apple was better? I didn't take you for a lemon meringue man. And look here. I was right."

"I didn't know I wore my pie preference on my sleeve," Ethan says, studying his forearms, like maybe it's there and he just doesn't know it.

The waitress laughs—a deep sound that fills the whole diner—and grabs the plate of lemon meringue. "Why don't I get you a slice of that apple, hmm? Best pie in the county. Guaranteed." She winks at Ethan. "On the house."

Ethan tips an invisible hat. "I can't refuse."

"Jeez," I say, once the waitress is gone. "You're certainly Prince Charming out here on the plains, aren't you?"

"Pft. No."

"Oh, come on. I bet the ladies love you."

I act like I'm teasing—and I am, mostly. But part of me really *does* want to know about this side of Ethan. Not that I think he's always hitting on waitresses, but he *is* charming.

And at six-four with Abercrombie looks, he must have a few girls in his recent past, or heck, in his present—we've just never talked about it.

"Hardly," Ethan says. "I think I bore the snot out of most of my dates. I literally talk about the weather all the time. It even happened to me in high school. Remember Abby Orland?"

I nod, thinking back to the curvy, dark-haired girl who stopped by to pick Ethan up sometimes. Ethan never did let her come in the apartment (thinking she'd get slurred at by Mom), but I know she and Ethan dated, and they even went to prom together. Ethan had showed me the photo of them standing in front of the cardboard ocean, his arm around her waist, both of them smiling.

"She dumped me because she said I paid more attention to the clouds than to her. Plus she was pissed I didn't get drunk with her after the prom. Or any other time. Also I think she was mad I didn't sneak her pizza when I had that job at Roberto's."

I grin. "She wanted free slices?"

"A free *pie* more like it. That girl could eat."

We're still laughing when the waitress brings my coffee, and I load it with cream and sugar. "It's hard, though," Ethan says, getting serious again, "being on the road for so much of the year. And even when we're not, there's lab work and research. And Polly. Cripes, what a project."

"Did Victor get any good data from her, from the chase?" I ask.

Ethan shakes his head. "I don't know yet. We only had her

on the ground for such a short time before the twister lifted. It's bittersweet, really. Patchy Falls gets a lucky break, but our data set gets the shaft."

The waitress stops by to drop off my French toast and Ethan's pie. "Enjoy," she says, refilling our coffee cups.

"Thanks," Ethan says, and we dig in.

After a few bites, Ethan sets down his fork. "I wanted to let you know, I go to some Al-Anon meetings down here. Have for a few years now. I was thinking maybe you'd like to join me for the next one? When we're back at my house, that is, not on the road."

French toast gets stuck in my throat. Cat's list has followed me.

Al-Anon is a support group for people affected by alcoholics, and I had no idea Ethan had ever set foot inside a meeting. I'd read about Al-Anon online, but I'd never imagined going. Even though I know Mom has a problem, I could *never* imagine airing my dirty laundry in front of a crowd. What if someone there knew me? But somehow, Ethan has been going—for *years*.

"I don't know." I busy myself stacking my creamers and folding my sugar packets into tiny squares. Al-Anon is for people who have no idea how to cope with alcoholics. Up until the accident, I thought I was coping just fine, thank you.

"My standoff with Mom? That came out of the Al-Anon meetings," Ethan continues. "I told her I would always love her and that she'd always be my mom. But I wanted her to get help. I encouraged her to admit she has a problem, and I told her I'd stand by her when she did."

"And when she didn't, you cut her off. Cut *us* off." The words come out hot and fast.

Ethan wipes his mouth with his napkin. "If that were true, really true, would you be here right now?"

I'm here because of Cat, I think. But I don't say that. I haven't told Ethan about that day, and I don't intend to. "I'm just here to figure a few things out," I reply, "and to work a summer job that doesn't have me washing dishes."

Ethan stares at me. "Good for you. And when the summer's over? You'll go back to . . . what, again? Remind me, because when I was seventeen and living in that apartment, all I can remember is grocery shopping and cleaning the bathroom and trying to keep you out of Mom's bedroom before eleven on a Saturday morning."

In my head I am counting backward from ten so I don't lose it on Ethan right there and then. "No family is perfect," I say. "But call me crazy, I thought families were supposed to stick together. Not *abandon* each other." *Who do you think had to start cleaning the bathroom once you were gone?*

Ethan rubs his forehead. "I left to build a life for myself, Jane. I got a scholarship to the University of Oklahoma. You think I wasn't going to take it? I wanted to start *doing* something instead of cleaning up after Mom. You should start thinking about that, too. About the future. You know?"

"I can think about the future without *deserting* people," I fire back. "Mom isn't perfect, but she's our mom. Except all you do is focus on the bad stuff, even though our childhood was totally normal. I mean, considering she had to raise us solo since Dad only came around to knock her up twice and disappear, she did okay. She bought us costumes for Halloween, and most years we had Christmas presents under the tree. You remember how we used to make Wonder Bread sandwiches and toast them over the stove? Why don't you ever focus on *that* stuff?"

Ethan leans in, gets close to me. "Because Mom has a problem," he says. "She's an alcoholic. And no matter what else she is, she's that first. She's addicted to a drug, and she'll do anything to get it. It defines her. It defines *life* with her. Do you understand that?"

I swallow the pinpricks in my throat. I don't let myself think for a second he could be right, because nothing in this world is that black and white.

"No," I say. "She's still more than her drinking. You can't just look at it like that. And for the record, she went to rehab after you left. But you never seem to take *that* into account."

"Oh, right," Ethan says, smacking his forehead. "My gosh, how could I have forgotten how she half-assed that one attempt at sobriety when I threatened to call Social Services on her? And then when I didn't, she went right back to her old habits. How stupid of me."

My heart slams into my ribs. "You threatened her?"

"Hell, yes, I did. To try and make things better for you. Force her to clean up. But I could never make that call, because then what if you got shipped off to some awful foster home? I couldn't live with myself if you landed in some family where they treated you even worse. Took advantage of you or—God, I don't know. Mom called my bluff, kept on drinking, and I did jack."

"You *manipulated* her?" I ask, hardly believing what I'm hearing. "And when she couldn't do it, you *blamed* her?"

"You say that like she deserves a medal for her one pathetic attempt. The stakes for which were losing *you*, I might add. If I were a parent, I might try harder than that."

"Jesus, *nothing's* good enough for you!" My anger is boiling over, spilling out between us in hot waves I can practically feel.

At the other end of the counter, the waitress looks up from where she's wiping down glassware with a gingham cloth.

"You know what," Ethan says, dropping his voice, "let's stop talking about what's good enough for me and talk about what's good enough for you. This supposed life you have with Mom? No way that should be good enough for you."

"Don't tell me wh—"

Ethan doesn't let me finish. "It's just a theory, but I'd be willing to put money on the idea that somewhere inside, you *are* taking a good, hard look at your life. I think that's part of the reason you're here. Maybe something happened. Maybe Mom's really losing it over her dead brother. Hell, maybe she's not, and you just decided to come to Oklahoma for a summer to see me. But I think there's a wheel turning in your brain that keeps squeaking at you. And the more it turns, the louder it squeaks, and it's telling you that something isn't right. That *Mom* isn't right. That there's more to life than a dingy apartment in Minnesota with her."

The accident. Uncle Pete. The hours at Larry's. The disappearing money. The calls into work. Were those all squeaking at me?

Okay, yes. Of course. I wasn't blind enough not to admit that much. But the answer couldn't be to run away like Ethan did. Or to do all the things on Cat's list and let my mom wind up in a cardboard box somewhere. The answer was to figure out how to make life better. To make sure the same mistakes didn't keep happening over and over.

Right?

"Things are fine," I say. "Mom and I are fine." No thanks to you. "You can go to all the meetings you want, but I'm the one who knows how things are up there. Not you."

Ethan shrugs. "Suit yourself."

How can he be so oblivious? I want to toss my cold coffee in his face and wake him up. I want him to admit I'm right. That he screwed up by leaving us. That he's sorry. That he's coming back.

The waitress drops off our check. There's a big fat question mark behind her eyes, like, *everything okay here?*

"Thanks," Ethan says, reassuring her with a smile that shows all his straight, white teeth. I scowl as she walks away.

I pull a crumpled ten-dollar bill from my pocket for the check. Ethan waves it away. "I got this," he says. "My treat."

"No, let me pay my share."

Ethan pulls the tab closer. "Nope. Not this time."

I stuff my money back into my pocket. I don't know why, but Ethan paying feels like a power move. Like he's trying to prove how completely awesome he is. When, really, it's only pie and French toast. It doesn't make him Captain Amazing.

Maybe it's the expression on my face or the way I'm balling my fists, but it doesn't take Ethan long to figure out I'm pissed.

"Hey," he says, putting a hand on my shoulder. "I'm just trying to help you. Okay?"

I know he's talking about more than the tab. I know he's trying to do what he thinks is best for me. Just like Cat.

But how can they both be so confident they know what's right when they're not *in* it? They don't live it. They don't know how it *is*.

"You want a trophy or something?" I ask, and hurt flashes across Ethan's face, but only for a second. When the bill is paid, we leave and head back to the motel, the plains flat and silent all around us.

14

The next morning, we all gather in the lobby at seven to hit Happy's for breakfast because we're sick to death of motel buffets.

The front desk is empty, and I'm leaned against it, trying to stay awake while we wait for Victor. Of course *he'd* be late. Ethan and Stephen are parked nearby in wide, overstuffed plaid chairs that have—get this—built-in ashtrays in the armrests. Ethan had nodded at me when I came into the lobby, but he didn't say anything. For my part, I barely looked at him.

To my right, Mason is leaning against a rack of brochures. He's thumbing through a pamphlet for the Kool-Aid museum in Hastings, Nebraska.

"Whoa, that is *amazing*," Hallie says, sidling up to me and pointing to the metal owl hanging around my neck on a long chain. "Where in the world did you get it?"

"I can't remember," I hedge, because the answer is a dingy

flea market on the outskirts of Minnetonka Mills. It was all of twenty-five cents.

"I wish I could pull off wearing something like that," Hallie says. "I'd give anything for some style." I bite my lip at that because girlfriend is wearing jeans with a thick silver belt buckle in the shape of a horse head. On anyone else it would look ridiculous, but on Hallie it's the perfect mix of glamour and cowgirl.

"Yar, methinks there's only one style to have," Mason pipes up. "High-seas swashbuckling attire!" Hallie and I both turn. Mason's speaking like it's International Talk Like a Pirate Day, which he does a lot, even though the official "holiday" is in September.

"So where's your ruffled shirt and boots?" I ask, playing along.

"Arrr, they be at the dry cleaners."

"They have dry cleaners in pirating, huh?"

"Aye. Ishmael opened a chain after the whaling business didn't turn out so good for him."

I laugh until I notice Mason's face is suddenly pale and his smile is gone.

"Hey, what's wrong?" I ask. "You okay?"

I follow the direction of Mason's gaze and see one of the motel's employees enter the other side of the lobby. She's short with curly brown hair. Cute, for sure. "I saw her last night," Mason says, his voice suddenly low. "She helped me get my change out of the vending machine. I—I tried to get her to play the vortex game with me."

Hallie and I glance at each other. "How did it go?" Hallie asks.

"I tried to pick a good setup. Like, one that could really spark conversation. So I said: if Captain Kirk or Admiral Adama got sucked into a twister and only one of them could survive, which would you choose?"

My eyes widen. "You led with *Star Trek* and *Battlestar Galactica*?"

"I know, right?" Mason's light brown eyes are flooded with regret. "I realize it was dumb. But at the time I just thought—I figured maybe she'd seen the shows before."

I'm almost afraid to ask the next question, but I do. "So what'd she say?"

"Nothing," Mason says, crossing his freckled arms. "She had no idea what I was talking about. She just got my money out of the machine and told me to have a good night."

"Aw, Mason," Hallie says, "I'm sorry. That sucks."

Mason shrugs. "It's how it goes, you know? The assholes always get the girl, while the nice guy who can calculate horizontal velocities in his head just gets his change back."

I stare at him. "You can calculate horizontal velocities in your head?"

"Yeah. But it doesn't do much for me. Apart from weather, I mean."

"Jeez," I say, "sorry, man."

Mason looks genuinely hurt. "I'm beginning to wonder if I'll be single forever. Maybe I'm just going to wind up like those dudes who only ever date in Second Life."

"That's not true," I say, knowing Mason deserves better than a love life with online avatars. For the right girl, Mason's a catch. He's smart, he's kind, and he's not afraid to sing *Oklahoma!*—in Kansas. Or wherever.

"Thanks," Mason says, but I can tell he's not convinced.

Just then, Victor saunters into the room—finally.

Ethan and Stephen pull themselves out of their plaid smoking chairs. "Now that we're all here," Stephen says, smoothing his huge beard, "I wanted to update you on the Patchy Falls situation. I was able to speak with Alex last night, and the Twister Blisters are going to stay put for a few days. I think, based on what happened last night, that it's smart if we join them in cleaning up the town."

The hairs on the back of my neck stand up. *Max.* His plan worked, and now we'll be sticking around Patchy Falls together.

"It's not for very long," Stephen says, "and I imagine we'll be chasing again in no time. But while we're here, we're going to be around a lot of cameras. Which means that after breakfast I need each of you to head to the Weather Network trailer in Patchy Falls and sign a waiver saying you give them permission to record you."

My stomach drops. Waiver or no, the idea of being on television is terrifying.

"What if we don't want them filming us?" Victor asks. "What if we think the plan is bullshit?"

Stephen folds his arms. "This is the only way it works, Vic. You of all people have the most to gain by complying with the release."

Victor just scowls.

"So after breakfast," Stephen continues, ignoring Victor's glares, "we'll head to Patchy Falls, sign the paperwork, then we'll coordinate with the other volunteer crews. I want everyone to pitch in and do whatever's needed, okay? And if there's a Weather Network camera around, smile while you do it. Got it?"

We all nod, and Stephen seems satisfied. "Okay, then," he says. "Let's go get some grub."

"Here," Hallie says, handing me a pair of work gloves. "You're going to need these." I eye a two-by-four sprouting rusty nails and think maybe it's not such a bad idea.

"Thanks." I take the gloves and slide them on. Within nanoseconds, my hands are sweating. I squint up at the sun. It's barely ten o'clock in the morning and already it must be at least ninety degrees. Cleaning up Patchy Falls today is going to be a bitch. I wish suddenly that Jersey Street, where we are and where Patchy Falls was hardest hit, had more trees to shade us. And then I realize it probably did—before the storm snapped them like toothpicks and sent them sailing into the next county.

Farther down the block, a cluster of people heave branches out of the road, and I crane my neck for a good look at them. I'm hoping one of them is Max.

"Looking for someone?" Hallie asks.

I whip back to attention. "No," I say quickly. Too quickly.

"You sure about that?"

Hallie will be a junior next year at the University of Oklahoma, so we're only a few years apart. And while she's cool and an awesome chaser, I'm not exactly ready to be besties and go blabbing to her about Max.

"It's nothing," I say.

I wipe a rivulet of sweat off my forehead and bend down to grab the two-by-four. Hallie picks up the other end and helps me. After we heave the thing into a nearby Dumpster, we stare at each other. A small smile plays at the corner of her mouth.

"So, you're not looking for anyone?" she asks. "Not one single person? Not a member of the Twister Blisters even?"

"Are you trying to make a point here?"

In the distance, a truck backs up with a series of shrill beeps.

"It's just that I saw you with one of the Blisters yesterday at breakfast," Hallie says. "Cute guy, dark hair? Thought maybe you guys hit it off or something. And since the Blisters are in Patchy Falls too, maybe—"

"A Blister? No way." I try to end the conversation by scooping up an armful of leaves and tossing them into the Dumpster. Unfortunately, they're too light. They all come flying back at me, landing in my hair, on my face.

Hallie brays with laughter.

"It's not funny!" I say, but she's already doubled over. I giggle and whip a few leaves at her. She grabs a scrawny branch and thwaps it against my butt. I shriek and toss more leaves.

"You have to tell me!" she yells. "You're looking for someone out here. I know you are!"

"You know jack!"

"If it's not the breakfast boy, I bet it's one of the Weather Network guys. You're letting him get in your pants so they air more footage of you!"

I laugh harder. "Oh, my God, *no*."

"It's breakfast boy, then!" Hallie says, waving her wimpy branch at me. "I know it is!"

I stop our play fight to frantically peel the leaves out of my hair and brush the dirt off my shorts and shirt. I suppose she'll figure out everything she needs to know in the next few seconds. Danny's heading toward us—and Max is with her.

15

"Danny!" I say. I hope my voice doesn't betray how my insides are twisting at the sight of Max in jeans and a snug white T-shirt that shows off his broad shoulders. "You're on crutches!"

"Yeah," Danny says, smiling and looking at her ankle. "Just for a few weeks. Doctor says I have a sprain." Her wavy brown hair shimmers, the dirt and blood from last night long gone. There's a bright white bandage covering the gash on her forearm, plus a few bruises here and there, but other than that, she seems completely fine.

"Max here told me your name," Danny continues. "I asked around about you guys and finally found him. I had to thank you both in person for what you did for me last night."

I swallow back the guilt at how Victor—our own teammate—wanted to leave her injured in the darkness. She shouldn't be thanking me. Max, maybe—but not a Torbro.

"This is Hallie," I say, changing the subject. "She's a chaser, too."

Hallie pulls off a glove and extends her hand. "Nice to meet you. Glad to see you're up and about."

Danny nods. "The doctors kept me overnight, but released me first thing this morning. My boyfriend took me home, and—would you even believe it?—I came in the door, and there was a pile of food there for me. Casseroles, cakes, even a whole roast turkey from the ShopRite. It's like I was gone for a month with a terminal illness."

"Must be nice to have neighbors who care about you so much," Max offers. It's the first time he's spoken since they walked up. I try not to stare at the way his mouth moves.

"You bet," Danny agrees. "We do take care of our own 'round here. But I have to tell you, the whole town is powerful thankful you chasers stuck around after the storm. I suppose it could have been much worse. Good Shepherd Lutheran lost most of its roof and windows. The Johnsons lost half a garage. No one died, though, and no one lost *everything*. For the mess that is here, well, we're just really grateful you're helping out."

And helping ourselves *out,* I think. Good thing Danny doesn't know this is a PR stunt for both teams as much as it is a humanitarian effort.

"Do you need anything?" Max asks, like he's thinking the same thing and wants to get the focus off the chasers. "Is there something we can help you with?"

"I'd ask if you know where I can get a deal on a new chasing van, but I think I'll be laying off the storms for a while."

"Storms are hard to predict," Max agrees. "The Twister

Blisters get mixed up all the time, and we've got Doppler and a team of six."

Danny nods. Down the block, a chain saw starts up. "Well, I need to get back home, and I'm dropping Max here off at the Culvers' barn. Guess it got hit by some winds and his team's gonna fix it up."

I fight down a wave of disappointment when I hear that Max won't be helping Hallie and me for the rest of the day. "But if you're around tonight," Danny continues, "I wanted to invite you all out to the Pig & Spit over in Clarkstown. The Bluegrass Aces are playing there tonight raising money for Pastor Kraus and the Good Shepherd. Lots of people have been asking if the chasers might come too. Chasers are the closest thing we have to celebrities around here."

"I'll be there," Max says. His eyes are boring into mine, willing me to say I'll go. To decide right then and make it happen.

"Okay, cool," I agree.

Danny smiles. "It really will be a good time." She looks at Max. "You ready to go?"

Max flashes a grin at Hallie and me. "Good to see you," he says. His electric green eyes linger on mine for a second.

"Good to see *you*," Hallie replies, elbowing me.

We stand there watching Danny and Max climb into a black truck parked a little ways off. After the diesel engine rumbles to life and they drive away, Hallie faces me.

"So, *Max* was nice."

I shrug. "He's okay."

"Seems like he was more than just *okay*. Seems like he was *olé*, as in that bull can run through my red cape any time." Hallie cracks up at her own joke. I go back to picking up branches and try to ignore her. "Though I have to tell you," Hallie continues, "it would be really hard dating someone on a rival chasing team. You'd probably have to clear it with the other chasers, you know. Have a meeting. Come clean on both sides. Make sure *everyone* knew."

I straighten. "Don't you dare," I say. "Don't say anything to anyone."

Hallie bursts into laughter. "I knew it! Oh, my God, you should see your face!"

"This isn't funny," I protest, imagining a powwow with both teams talking about whether two rival chasers could date. Romeo and Juliet—only with consensus. And bad weather.

"Come on, Jane. Lighten up, buttercup. Who am I going to tell? Stephen? Your brother?"

"Maybe," I say. "I don't know."

Hallie makes like she's locking her lips shut. "Your secret is safe with me," she says, tossing away the imaginary key. "But you might want to practice not staring at Max in public before you go to the Pig & Spit tonight."

"You're coming too, right?"

"Oh, hell, yes," she says. "I wouldn't miss this for the world."

16

I smooth down my hair as best I can and grab my room key. Just as I'm ready to head to the Pig & Spit, my phone buzzes. I look at the caller ID: Cat.

It's funny how we used to talk on the phone every day, but now a phone call from her feels like this ginormously huge deal. I take a deep breath. On the third ring, I hit Talk.

"Hey, Cat."

"Hey," she says, her voice as even as mine. "I wanted to call and see how you're doing."

"I'm great," I say. "Really good. You?"

"I'm fine." I can practically see her sprawled on her pink comforter, magazines spread around her in glossy, overlapping waves. I miss her so much in that moment, my chest tightens. "Are you guys, uh, seeing many storms?"

I can hear how hard she's trying to make conversation. "Actually, we are," I say, working to give her more than two-word answers, since she *did* make the effort to call. "Right now, we've stopped in this town called Patchy Falls to help them clean up after a twister."

"Really? That sounds pretty cool."

"It's—yeah, I guess it is. There's this other chase team, the Twister Blisters, and they're here too. They have Weather Network cameras following them around all the time, and when we come into contact with the Blisters, we sometimes wind up getting filmed."

"Are you going to be on TV?" Cat asks, sounding excited.

"I don't know. My brother probably will be. And definitely this guy named Victor. He's on our team, but secretly storms wig him out."

"No way. How can you be a chaser and not love storms?"

"I know, right?" I say, my words coming more quickly now. "And you know what this guy did? After the tornado hit Patchy Falls, we were trying to help people, but Victor was so scared of another storm rolling in that he left this one injured woman. He just, like, ran away from her."

"For real?"

"Totally for real."

"I just can't imagine," Cat says, "why someone would *do* that. It sounds like he needs some serious help. I mean, he's putting people in danger, you know? Because he can't face . . ."

Cat trails off and I suddenly realize she's afraid to go on, afraid of how much the Victor situation sounds like *my* situation. Or my situation as Cat sees it, anyway.

I swallow. No *way* am I like Victor.

"I didn't mean for that to come out the way it did," Cat says finally. "I wasn't calling to bring anything up, I was only calling to see how you were. Really. And to tell you in person that I'm proud of you for going down to live with your brother for the summer. I know it was hard."

I don't tell her how my brother wants me to stay with him permanently. I don't tell her how he wants me to go to Al-Anon too. But I do tell her at least part of the truth. "I'm pretty confused," I admit. "About all this. About what I'm supposed to do to help my mom. I don't even know what to think anymore."

"Oh, Jane. I can't imagine how awful—how hard this is."

It's nice that right then Cat doesn't try to tell me what to do. She's just in it with me. "Thanks," I say.

"Look, I'm here, okay? I know my note was tough. But I'm not sitting here saying you have to do all these things right now, this second. It's a process. A journey . . . or something."

"Thanks, I guess," not sure what to say. I reach for more of the truth. "I'm glad you called."

"Me too."

We make a plan to talk again in a couple weeks. When we hang up, I'm standing in front of the dusty motel mirror, and instead of turning away, I stare—really stare—at the girl in the reflection.

I've gained weight on the road, and even though it's from eating fast food and sitting too much, it's rounded out my sharp edges. My blue eyes are brighter, and being out in the sun has bronzed my skin. My copper-and-straw hair is still a wavy mess, but it's lighter now.

I take a breath. Was I really so hungry and pale and stressed before this? I wish it didn't take me leaving my mom to look more like a happy teenager. I wish everything could just be normal back home. I can all but hear my mom laugh: *If wishes and buts were candy and nuts, we'd all have a merry Christmas.* Even by my mom's definition, there's no use sitting around hoping for things that will never be.

The Pig & Spit is loud, hot, and crowded, but even so, I can spot the chasers immediately. They're the ones with the cameras trained on their table. I know at least one lens is zooming in on me now as I cut through a bank of cigarette smoke to reach the table. I'm the last one to arrive.

Ethan waves at me. "Jane! We thought you'd been sucked into a tornado!" He's smiling, our fight at Happy's apparently forgotten.

"If I had, would you chase it?"

Ethan shakes his head. "And leave the Pig & Spit? No way."

Next to Ethan, Hallie pipes up. "Hey, Jane!" she says. She jerks her head toward the other end of the table. "I made sure you had a seat. Down *there*." At the very end of the long table is one empty seat. Next to Max. Hallie winks at me, and I try not to blush as I make my way to the chair.

Max is to my left. Directly across the table is Mason, flanked by two of the tech guys from the Twister Blisters. From the bits of conversation I catch above the din of country music, they're absorbed in a discussion about multiple vortices, meaning a bunch of tornadoes at once. To my right, unfortunately, is Victor.

"You missed the appetizers," Max says when I'm finally parked. "Pieces of deep-fried steak you dunk into gravy." I don't mind the fact that he has to lean in close so I can hear him.

"Uh, yum?"

"Crazy stupid delicious," Max says, locking eyes with me. A funnel cloud forms in my spine. "For dinner we all ordered the ribs," Max continues. "Well, most everyone. I think Mason got the fried chicken, and one of the Blisters got a hamburger. But the waitress said the ribs were the best."

"Place like this, I'm not surprised," I say.

A waitress walks past. "Want something, hon?" she asks.

Victor grunts, and drains his beer. "'Nother," he says, interrupting my order. I'm about to mumble "jerk" under my breath, but the word dies on my lips when I get a good look at him. He's unshaven, and his face is crisscrossed with lines I've never noticed before. He seems exhausted. I don't want them to, but my insides twist for him. It must be awful, I realize, being terrified of bad weather and watching yourself turn into a monster on chases as a result.

"Honey? You want something or not?" The waitress taps her pen against her notepad. I tear my eyes away from Victor.

"Yes, um, the ribs," I say. "And a Diet Coke, please."

"You got it."

"So what'd you do the rest of the day?" Max asks. He leans an elbow against the table and gets that much closer. I feel a cold thrill, even in the hot restaurant.

"More Dumpster duty," I say. "Hot, sweaty, stupid Dumpster

duty." I roll my eyes, but I'm smiling. It wasn't so bad—not with Hallie there, and it felt good to help Patchy Falls, even if we did it to save our own asses in the process. "You?"

Max whispers in my ear, so the Weather Network cameras won't pick up on our conversation. The minute I feel his breath on my lobe, I take a sip of the Diet Coke the waitress has set in front of me, so I don't haul off and kiss him right there. "We went out to rebuild a barn for this old couple. Your brother and Stephen were there, too. So was a Weather Network producer, and he got pushy about stuff. Like, making your brother and Stephen take their shirts off because they're both so ripped. I mean, it's smart, because it's going to be a total ratings fest when the episode airs. But it feels so fake. There is nothing 'real' about reality TV. Nothing whatsoever."

I glance down the table and, as if to confirm what Max is saying, I see one of the camera operators talking to Stephen, Ethan, and Alex. He motions with his hands and, a moment later, the three guys clink their glasses together. They make it look spontaneous—as if the two rival teams have put aside their differences to clean up Patchy Falls. "See what I mean?" Max asks. Then, to my amazement, they do it *again*—this time with Hallie in the scene. I try not to throw up when I see Alex weasel in closer to her.

A waitress interrupts the setup by bringing over a tray of shots to that end of the table. "From table twelve!" she says. Danny and four other women at a nearby booth wave at the chasers.

Ethan shakes his head at his shot and offers it to Hallie. She grins and throws back the brown liquid, one then another. I never figured Hallie for a drinker, but any girl who can take two shots like that and not get sick has to have had some practice at it. I see she's got a beer in front of her as well.

The food arrives, and I stop thinking about Hallie and the cameras. I'm so ravenous, I don't even wait until everyone is served before digging in. The sweet, saucy ribs are perfect, and I'm almost inhaling them. There's also buttered corn, steaming rolls, and fluffy mashed potatoes on the side. The whole table goes quiet as everyone chews and swallows. It's the closest thing we've had to home-cooked food in a long time.

The Bluegrass Aces start playing about the time I'm so stuffed I feel like I might explode. "We got a basket up here," the bass player says, his long, gray beard touching the mic, "for Pastor Kraus and some of the folks whose homes were damaged in the twister. If you can throw a buck or two in while you do-si-do past, we'd sure appreciate it." A cheer goes up from the bar, and the band plays a few notes then quiets again. The bass player continues, "And let's have a round of applause for the Twister Blisters and the Tornado Brothers, who stuck around after the storm to help us out. Three cheers for them!"

Every pair of eyes in the place turns to our table, and all I can think about is ducking under my chair to hide. I feel like there's a neon sign above us flashing POSEURS. Nevertheless, I smile along with the other chasers and hope the good folks of this town have heard one of my mom's other favorite expressions: *There's no such thing as a free lunch.*

The Bluegrass Aces start a song that includes both a fiddle

and a banjo, and half of the Pig & Spit gets up to dance. I'm so full, I want to put my head down on the table and nap, but suddenly there's a hand on my shoulder. It's Ethan. "C'mon," he says. "Time to dance." I want to protest, but then I see the cameras. So I get up and follow him to the scuffed-wood dance floor, crowded and sticky with spilled drinks. Everyone smiles and makes room for us.

Ethan puts his hands on his hips and moves his legs in a weird sort of shuffle skip. I look around and, to my horror, realize everyone else is doing the same thing. Except me. I have no idea what song the band is playing and no idea how to dance to it.

"It's a line dance," Ethan hollers above the noise. "Just do what I do." I can feel myself begin to sweat, but I try to look like I'm having the time of my life, knowing the cameras are probably zoomed in on my shiny face and Max is likely out there somewhere watching. Ethan backs up a few steps, then leans forward. By the time I lean, everyone else is on to the next move, and I wind up bumping into a woman wearing a cowboy hat as wide as she is. Which is saying something.

"Sorry!" I manage. Ethan laughs, and I glare at him.

"Side to side!" he says, and crosses one leg over the other. I do the same—until everyone starts going the other direction. This time, I crash into a man with a handlebar moustache, who reaches out a steadying hand.

"Easy there, little filly."

I can't even look at him, I'm so embarrassed. I hear a roar and realize Ethan is almost bent over, he's laughing so hard.

He's all but given up dancing. The crowd is sashaying and do-si-do-ing all around us. I smack his shoulder, which only makes him laugh harder.

"You did this on purpose!" I say.

Ethan is helpless. Tears are coursing down his cheeks.

I want to be mad, but seeing Ethan laugh so hard, I can't help it. I laugh too. "Where did you learn to line dance?" I ask.

Ethan wipes the tears away. "I live in Oklahoma, Jane," he says. He's still grinning. "It's practically a national pastime down here."

My smile vanishes. I don't want to, but I can't help but think that while Mom and I have been struggling in Minnesota, Ethan's been *line dancing*.

"Come on," he says, "this next one's a lot easier. And look, we have company."

Max and Hallie squeeze onto the dance floor, followed by Stephen and Mason. One of the locals with fire-red cowboy boots tries to dry-hump Hallie to the beat of the music before she makes a scissors with her right hand and hollers something about his balls. He backs off.

Some of the Pig & Spit locals go back to their tables to make room for us. With the camera crew, we've taken up a good chunk of the dance floor.

A manic fiddle starts up, and both Hallie and Ethan know what to do instantly. I watch Hallie kick her feet and spin, her face getting more and more flushed. Her skin has that same sheen my mom's gets when she drinks, but she's smiling and laughing, her eyes bright.

Suddenly, Max is next to me on the dance floor. He grabs one hand, and my legs wobble. He takes my other hand and leads me in a little two-step, then spins me around. Somehow, it doesn't surprise me that he knows exactly what to do. The warm lights and dark wood of the Pig & Spit swirl by. I tilt my head back and let my hair fly. I close my eyes. It takes me a moment to realize what I'm feeling: *I'm having fun.*

I stop spinning only to find Max smiling at me. His green eyes are shining, even in the dim space. I want to reach out and touch his hair—and I surprise myself by actually doing it. His eyes dart around, and I follow them. They find the cameras, which are trained on Hallie and Ethan, who are still dancing. Hallie wobbles slightly, tipsy, but it doesn't matter. She and Ethan are *in* this moment, moving as if the music is in their blood. Their energy fills the space around them. They're breathtaking.

"Come on," Max says. "Let's get out of here."

He pulls me to the side of the dance floor, straight into the crowd. My heart pounds, wondering where we're going and if we'll be caught. We slip past torsos and elbows, away from the cameras, weaving through the crush of people. When the front door comes into view, Max grips my hand even harder. "Now!" he says, and we make a break for the exit.

17

The Pig & Spit door closes behind Max and me, sealing in its heat and noise. Outside, in the cool of the night, crickets are chirping and stars blanket the sky.

At the edge of the Pig & Spit parking lot, Max keeps his grasp on my hand. "This way," he says. "I know where we can go."

I let him lead the way into the tall grass. I step behind him and wish I could hit the Pause button on this moment. That I could lie on my back in this sea of rustling green and float away with Max holding my hand and happiness gripping my heart.

Max and I walk for what feels like miles, but I don't mind. The grass is high, though we can still see over it. The two of us are quiet, letting the summer night make its sounds all around us.

Finally, Max points straight ahead. "We're here." I squint, and in the darkness, I see a looming shape.

"What is that?"

"The barn we worked on today," Max says. It's skeletal—mostly two-by-fours and a few sheets of plywood. I can smell new lumber and sawdust.

Max threads his way through the beams to the center of the barn, and I tag behind. "We were working on the loft today. We can get up there if I can just find the—" He stops. "Eureka," he says, and starts to climb the ladder he'd apparently been looking for. "Normally I'd say ladies first," he calls down, "but in this case, I think I'd better head up in front of you. Hold on a sec." I lose sight of him in the blackness. There's shuffling on what I can only imagine is a platform above. "Okay," he says after a second. "It's safe for you to come on up if you want."

Slowly, I ascend the ladder behind him until I'm out in the open in the barn's half-built hayloft. There's nothing but a few scant roof beams above us, and nothing but grass and sky everywhere else.

"Pretty cool, huh?" Max asks.

There are no words for how small I feel. And, yet, I want to tell Max that I still feel special because I'm here with *him*. But I don't want to sound like a lameass, so I just say "Awesome." I pause. "Did we just walk all the way to Patchy Falls?"

"Not quite. The barn's a lot closer to Clarkstown than you'd think. We only walked a mile or so."

I inhale air filled with the smell of lumber and earth. The plains are so flat, I feel like I can see all the way to the Pacific.

"This is something," I say, and mean it.

Max sits down on the rough floor, then pats it with his hand.

"Have a seat," he says. I join him, wondering how close I can get before it's obnoxious. I settle for having our knees touch.

"I'm a regular here, by the way. The bartender knows me." Max waves with his hand. "Beer and a shot, please."

"Make that two," I add, even though in real life I'd just have Diet Coke.

Max turns to me. I can make out his face, his lips, his eyes. "I just realized something," I say. "I don't know your last name."

"Vaughn," he says. "Maximilian Adam Whittaker Vaughn, if you want the full version. But you can just call me Max."

I blink at how *rich* it sounds. It reminds me of *The Great Gatsby*—a movie I'd watched because I didn't feel like reading the book for class. So instead Mom and I popped popcorn and sat on the couch marveling at the sparkling champagne, glimmering jewels, and stupid excess.

"My online profile notes I'm six-one, seventeen years old. I'm a Sagittarius, and I like long walks on the beach."

I smile. "Very funny."

Max ticks more facts off his fingers. "I'm from Vermont. My favorite food is sushi, but the chicken-fried steak down here is a close second. I have one older brother. My dog's name is Boner, no lie. I named him when I was eight. I go to school in upstate New York at the Bartholomew Academy."

"Sounds fancy," I say, not just about the school, but about almost everything. I mean, whose favorite food is sushi?

"The academy's okay," Max says. "It's all guys, though, which sucks."

"Oh." I wonder if next he's going to tell me about his personal driver and how hard it is to have only an outdoor swimming pool and not an indoor one too.

"You okay?" Max says. "You got kinda quiet all of a sudden."

"Just, uh, wondering why you're out here in the middle of nowhere doing this internship."

Below us, a bullfrog starts its throaty croaking. "Weather is so totally badass. I saw these chases on the Weather Network and just knew I had to do it. Plus, I really dig the science. It's kind of a meld, you know? Physics and chemistry and math. Also it helps that my dad and Alex's dad go way back. So I had an in."

Makes sense that Max would be connected. People with that much money usually are.

"Not that knowing Alex is helping me," Max continues. "Pretty much I'm just a Sherpa, carrying Alex's shit around. But I'm trying to make the best of it, because supposedly this is the only summer I might ever be able to chase. After this, my dad says I need to use my school breaks to 'buckle down and start working for the family company.'"

"Which is?"

"Vaughn Commodities Management. We help people buy stuff abroad. For cheap."

"You sound like you hate it."

Max laughs. "I can't stand it. Which is why I know there's no way I'm doing it. If my dad pushes it, I'll probably drain my savings and hit the road for a while. Maybe come back down here and chase with a different team. Or I could hit Moab and just rock climb for a while."

"Where's Moab?" I ask, picturing the rocky coast of some far-off country.

"Utah."

I blush, embarrassed at how little I've traveled outside Minnesota. Max rolls past it. "So let's talk about you, Jane McAllister." He pretends like he's holding a microphone. "I need to ask you if you believe in a higher power, in the great mysterious, in fate, as it were." He points the make-believe microphone at me.

There's no way I believe in any of that stuff, but I play along. "Why do you ask?"

The microphone is gone. Max is stone serious. "I mean, if anyone had told me I'd meet a pretty girl at a Days Inn, who talks funny and takes kick-ass photographs, I would have told them they were smoking something. We're in the middle-of-nowhere Nebraska, after all, during a summer where the most exciting thing I've done so far—apart from watch some storms—is try to hunt down Alex Atkins's brand of hair gel. So I think that's the universe talking. That's fate."

I snort. "Fate? Come on. *You're* the one who sat next to me at breakfast. *You're* the one who encouraged me to get the Torbros to stick around Patchy Falls. *You're* the one who told me you'd be at the Pig & Spit like you were daring me not to come. So don't say this is fate, Max. This is you. One hundred percent *you*."

Max grins. "I never thought of it that way. But I did sort of lead the charge, didn't I?"

I marvel at his ability to manipulate his environment and not even know it. "You could say that."

"Well, apart from this irrefutable fact, I'm glad I've gotten to know you."

I smile. "Know me? You've been in my life for a matter of hours. You think you know me?"

Max leans back. "Granted, I don't know you *well*, but I know you some."

He sounds so sure. "Like what?"

"Well, first of all, from that unfortunate display at the Pig & Spit, I know you can't dance worth shit. Beyond that, I know you're good under pressure. You could have freaked out when you found Danny, but you didn't. Also, I know you care about your brother, and maybe all the Torbros, because you pitched the Patchy Falls plan to them, even though it meant you'd have to help clean up the town. And I'm going to guess you color within the lines a lot, because the look on your face when I pulled you out of the Pig & Spit made me wonder if you were going to ditch me and run back inside. But now that you're here, I think you're cool with it."

I shiver, suddenly afraid. I don't remember the last time anyone looked at me and tried to see me—really see me—the way Max does. It unnerves me. What if he gets too close and sniffs out the truth about my mom being a boozer? What if he finds out how we live, about how our power gets cut off? About how all my clothes are used? Someone who goes to private school and eats sushi could never understand that. If Max knew the truth about my life, he'd probably just laugh or, worse, feel sorry for me and want to pay for everything. Which is the last thing I need.

Max's eyes are on me. A crackle of electricity ignites my body.

Have your fun, I think. *Just don't let him get too close.*

A moment passes, then another. Slowly, Max leans forward. I feel his lips on mine, and my eyes close. Right then, it doesn't matter who's rich or who eats ramen. Everything about him is powerful and gentle at the same time. His arms wrap around my body, and my hands somehow find his neck, his face. We pull each other closer, and every nerve in my body feels like it's on fire. I have been kissed before, but never like this.

Max's lips part slightly, and mine do the same. His tongue inside my mouth makes fireworks of color burst behind my closed eyelids. We explore and taste each other again and again, until Max finally pulls away. I want more—I think I could survive on nothing but his mouth for weeks—but I try not to let it show too much.

"I should get you home," he says. "It's really late, and your brother might be wondering where you are." Reluctantly, I nod. I hate to agree with him, but he's probably right. "But maybe we can come out here tomorrow night. I think the farmer down the road might put his cattle into the next pasture over, and it's supposed to be quite a show."

I smile. "Sounds riveting."

I don't tell him that I have my own motel room and that we probably don't have to walk to an unfinished barn just to be together. The truth is, I'm not sure I'm ready to bring Max back to my room. I'd just had my first real make-out session and it had nearly done me in; my whole body might actually explode if I actually had sex.

"Come on," Max says, standing. He extends his hand, and I take it. With one final look at the stars and fields all around us, we climb down the ladder and make our way back into Clarkstown.

18

The motel lobby is deserted as I sneak back to my room—or so I think until I hear a groan from the corner. I jump what feels like six feet in the air. Victor leans forward, out of the shadows, and laughs. "Scared you," he says. I can barely see his face, the way his black hair falls forward.

"Cripes," I whisper. "What are you doing here?"

"Just resting," Victor says, looking at me with red-rimmed eyes. As I get closer to him, I catch the smell of whiskey. "Better question is, whad're *you* doing here?"

His words jumble together. He's trashed.

I look around, debating whether to leave him or give him a hand back to his room. I could let him suffer out here, but I figure if I help him, maybe he won't tell Ethan that I snuck back into the motel at three A.M. If he even remembers it.

Besides, it's not like I don't know what to do in these kinds of situations.

"I'm here to get you back to your motel room," I say, assessing whether I'm strong enough to pull him to his feet. It's easier with my mom, who's only about twenty pounds heavier than me. "Can you stand?"

Victor puts his hands on either side of the chair. "This is really nish of you," he says. "I didn' think you gave a shit."

"I don't," I reply.

Victor pushes himself up a few inches, then falls back into the chair. "Then jus' leave me," he says. He waves his hand clumsily. "Jus' go."

I roll my eyes. Why are drunks so dramatic all the time? My mom starts out giddy and bubbly, but then it always morphs into hyperbole. Everything from the television *never ever having one thing on that she wants to watch ever* to no one understanding her and what she's going through—not even me.

"Okay, try again," I say, holding out my hands. "I'll pull you up. Ready? On the count of three."

Victor clasps my hands with his. They're toaster-oven hot.

"One, two, three—" I pull with all my strength and he comes lurching out of the chair. He stumbles forward but I catch him, or at least try to. He gets his footing and straightens.

"Thanks," he says, looking around. He blinks. "I got losh on the way to my room. I think it's thataway." He points at the doors leading outside.

"Do you know your room number?" I ask.

"Fifty eleven thousand," he says, then wheezes laughter.

"Very funny." I glance at the empty front desk. No one's on duty this late at night, which means Victor had better remember his room number, or he's going to be sleeping it off in the hallway.

"Do you have your key?" I ask. "Maybe in your pocket somewhere?"

Victor fumbles in his khaki shorts. After a bit, he pulls out a key with a plastic 108 tag on it.

"Awesome," I say, taking it from him. "Let's get you there."

"'Kay."

Victor shuffle-walks while I hold an arm to steady him. "Why are you doing thish?" he asks, wobbling slightly. "I've bem a dick to you."

We get to the vending machine, and I prop him up against a wall. "Hold that thought," I say, and feed a couple dollars in for bottled water. Victor's going to need to hydrate before bed. "Here," I say, handing him one. "Drink this."

He brings the bottle to his lips, misses a little, then tries again. He gets a few sips down. His scar rises and falls as he swallows.

"Can you drink and walk?" I ask. Victor nods, and we keep going.

"You didn't asser my question," he says. "'Bout why you're helping me."

"Let's just say I have some practice at it," I reply.

"*You* drink?" Victor says, his black eyes finding mine.

"Me? No."

"Ethan then? Maaaan, I knew he couldn't be that much of a Boy Scout."

"Not him either," I say unlocking the room. "This is your

place, right?" I know it's the right room, but I ask anyway to keep him distracted.

I flip on the light, and we both take in the unmade bed, the spare change scattered on the floor, the damp towels on top of the shabby dresser. In one corner is a suitcase that looks like it erupted clothing.

"Yup, this is right," Victor says, and walks in to sit on the bed. He looks dazed, like he doesn't know what to do next.

"Do you have aspirin?" I ask. "Maybe in your suitcase somewhere?"

He scrunches his brow. "Adfil, maybe."

Advil. Right. I open the top zipper of his suitcase and, next to his razor and some hair gel, spot a small white bottle. I shake out two pills and hand them to him.

"Take these with one of the bottles of water. You'll thank me for it in the morning."

Victor lifts the bottle in a mock toast, then swallows the two pills while I watch. "Anything else, Nurse Ratched?" he asks.

"Who?"

Victor gives me a lopsided smile. "Nurse Ratched. *One Flew Over the Cuckoo's Nes'*. Tell me you've seen it?"

"Sorry," I say, glancing at the same ancient clock radio on Victor's nightstand that's on mine—3:12 A.M. "Let's take your shoes off and call it a night."

"No, really," Victor says, as I unlace his dust-covered Converse. "You gotta see this movie. 'S amazing. Jack Nichols'n is sick. I mean, sick like awesome. Not sick like sick. Which is sort of the point." He pauses as I wrestle with his second shoe.

"Movies are so badass. I love them more than anything." I set his shoes by the bed. "Except one movie," he continues. "You know the movie I hate? *Twister*. I fucking hate that movie."

My stomach sinks. I have a feeling I know where this is headed.

"More than that," Victor says, his dark eyes shining, "I hate storms. Fuck storms forever. If we play the vortex game and you put something up against a storm, I'll take the other thing every time. A pile of dog shit. A rotting corpse. Drowning. I'll take it. I'll never choose the storm. *Never*."

"Okay, Victor," I say. "It's cool. We won't chase again for a while, so—"

"No!" he says. "Don't you get it? I'm a chaser and piss my pants about *storms*. I'm goddamn afraid of them." He sets down the water and presses his palms against his brow.

I sit in the ratty chair next to the bed. I can't leave now, with Victor in full rant. "And then I just left that Patchy Falls lady," Victor continues. "I can't shake it, you know? And I'm mean to Hallie just because she's a girl, and I shit all over Ethan when I can. Just because . . . because I'm so *unhappy*."

"So why do you chase if you hate storms?" I ask.

Victor won't raise his head. "Polly. She's our meal ticket. All the grant money's 'cuz of her. Something happens in the field, and she breaks, who's going to fix her?"

"Mason could probably handle it."

"Mason's all right, but I'm the one who built her. And now? *Now* we've got this bet. Alex Atkins called me out, so no way I can leave the team. I leave, and they get Polly anyway."

I'm still trying to figure out what to say when Victor lurches off the bed and stands above me. The scar on his face is suddenly deeper, angrier. I pull myself into the chair, my insides quaking. What if he's a raging drunk? What if he's about to hit me and I never saw it coming?

But instead, Victor fumbles in his back pocket and pulls out his wallet. "Here," he says, yanking out a battered photo, "lookit."

He shoves the creased image at me. It's a picture of Stephen around twelve years old. He's wearing cutoff jean shorts and a striped shirt, and his lanky frame is standing in front of a long, white tornado that's snaking across an ebony sky. The photo is straight-on, no nonsense. Accurate, not artistic. "You know who took that picture?" Victor asks, tapping the image over and over with a long finger. "Me. I did. I was there, but you'd never know it, would you?"

Victor's staring at me and I realize he wants an answer. "No," I reply honestly. "You wouldn't."

"Stephen's the weather boy *wondurr* who'd chase storms on his bike, for God's sake. All while I'd be riding along with him, trying to pull him back every time he got too close." He snatches the picture and shoves it back into his wallet.

I open my mouth, then close it. Victor sits back on the bed.

"Not that it was so bad. I liked mechanics. Parts. Stephen would get us to the storm, and I'd figure out a way to docu-men' it. I'm not a chaser. I'm an *engineer*. Always have been. But when we started the Torbros, that line got blurred. I wen' along with it, probably because deep down I was still thinking

I had to keep my little brother out of trouble. He tol' me one time he wouldn't chase if I wasn't there with him."

Victor looks so crushed. If I were braver, I might reach out and pat him on the back or something. But I don't dare.

"I bet everyone would understand," I offer, trying to fill the silence. "If you had to quit—"

"No way. 'Specially not after last season, when Stephen had to save the whole van full of us because of me. Talk about ironic. I fucked them once by putting them in danger. How can I sit here and think about fucking them all over again by giving Polly away?"

"But you can't stay in this life if it makes you *unhappy*," I protest. "I mean, does Stephen know how you feel?"

Victor shrugs. "He figures I'll snap out of it."

"You have to tell him all this," I insist. "Sticking around isn't good for you or the team. And you can't live your life for someone else. You need to—"

I stop. The rest of the words are stuck in my throat.

"What?" Victor says, looking at me with weary eyes. "Whaddew I need to do?"

I'm about to tell Victor to do the same things that everyone is telling *me* to do.

Live your own life. If you leaving means Stephen and the rest of the team have to struggle for a bit, so be it. It's all for the best.

The blood drains from my face. *Is it possible that I really am just like Victor?* Is it possible that we are nearly the same person, only instead of acting like a douche on chases and putting people in danger during storms, I'm acting like a douche and putting people in danger in the middle of intersections, inches from getting rammed by semis? All because I can't see the plain and simple fact that I have to stop living my life for someone else?

I think back to my recent phone call with Cat. Without even meaning to, she'd connected the dots between Victor and me. Just like nothing good could come of Victor living his life scared of storms for the supposed benefit of Stephen and the Torbros, nothing good could come of me working day and night for the supposed benefit of my mom.

Except that Stephen doesn't have a drinking problem, I think. And Stephen won't be living in a van down by the river if Victor no longer goes on chases. So it's different.

Except why does it feel the same?

Victor lies back on the bed and closes his eyes. "Fine if you don't want to tell me," he mumbles. "'Sokay. I've been a jerk. I s'pose I deserve it."

Victor's breathing slows, and I know he's inches away from a deep, drunk sleep.

"What if we have to hurt the people we love?" I ask. "What if that's the only way out?"

Victor just lets out a little snore. I pull the comforter over him as best I can and make sure the second bottle of water is on the bedside table. *I am Victor. Victor is me.*

I shake the thought and pull the door closed.

19

I launch out of bed the second I realize I've overslept. "Crap," I mumble, pulling on my work clothes from the day before. My mind is barely functioning, thanks to the late night with Max and Victor. Maybe with some coffee and food, I'll feel better.

I trot to the breakfast lounge to grab a granola bar and a to-go cup of joe before heading to town. I assume Hallie is on Jersey Street already, probably pushing a broom along the sidewalk, sweeping up debris. Which is why I'm surprised to see her nursing a glass of orange juice at one of the motel tables.

"Jane," she mumbles, tapping the glass with her fingers. She's wearing sunglasses indoors. "Yo."

I get a whiff of booze coming off her. "Are you—hungover?" I ask.

She nods. "In a bad way. Things got pretty wild at the bar last night. You know how it goes."

Actually, I don't. "How long were you there?"

Hallie shakes her head, then groans slightly. "Until closing."

Not wanting to stand there and pepper her with questions, I walk a few feet to the coffeemaker and pour myself a cup. Just to be nice, I get Hallie one too. I bring them both back to her table and sit.

"Are you going to go to Patchy Falls today?" I ask. "To work?"

She shrugs. "I don't know. I mean, I will if I can figure out how to stand up for five minutes without puking. But I was more hoping to talk to Ethan first. Things got a little weird last night."

I stiffen. "Weird how?"

I can see Hallie's eyebrows rise from behind her sunglasses. Like she just remembered that Ethan's not just a fellow chaser—he's my brother, too.

"Not *weird* weird. Just, you know."

It needles me that this is the second time Hallie has said "you know." Like I drink. Like I know what it's like to get wasted and wake up with a hangover. Like I understand what it means to pound back so much, I let stupid things happen with other people.

"Whatever it is," I say, "I'm sure Ethan will want to talk about it too."

"I hope so," Hallie agrees. "I mean, God, I hope he even remembers. We were both so wasted."

The coffee turns to ash in my mouth. I have to work to get it down. "Ethan doesn't drink."

"He let loose last night," Hallie says. "And then, I mean, I know he's your brother and all, but—I figure I'll just tell you—

we made out in my room. I'm sorry if that's awkward. He's this amazing guy, and I never thought about him that way before, but now I don't know. I think I might like him. But I don't want to act like a dumbass if he doesn't like me. So I was hoping to feel him out this morning. Not literally of course. Just, I mean, see where he stood on things." She pushes her orange juice away with a frustrated sigh.

My blood is pounding so hard, I can practically feel it in my fingertips. "You got my brother drunk?" I ask. "Then made out with him?"

Hallie pulls off her sunglasses and stares at me. The skin around her eyes is puffy and irritated. "Excuse me?"

"My brother doesn't drink," I say. "Not even a little. So if he was drunk, you must have done that to him."

"*Done that to him?* Jane, listen to yourself. What are you talking about? You think I forced shots down his throat, then took him back to my room or something?"

"I don't know," I say, standing. "But this isn't a game. We have—*problems* with this stuff in our family. So when I hear about my brother drinking, then doing stupid things, I get worried."

Hallie stands too. She rubs her temples. "Can we just take a step back for five seconds? Look, I know about your mom, and I understand things are fucked up with her. But that doesn't mean Ethan can't have a drink *ever*. And I don't appreciate you accusing me of 'doing things' to him, then also implying that any time he might have spent with me is stupid."

I clench my fists. I want to punch Hallie in her stupid scientific head if she thinks she understands anything about my mom, or how dangerous alcohol is to Ethan. Or me. The last thing I need is Ethan going off the edge too.

"Stay away from Ethan," I say, pushing back my chair, "and stay away from me."

Before she can reply, I march out of the breakfast room, hoping she spends the rest of the day bending over the toilet and throwing up her stupid hungover guts.

The day improves when I spot Max on Jersey Street. "What, no barn building today?" I ask.

"Hey, you," he says, leaning against the shovel he's using to pitch debris into a pile. "I was hoping I might catch you down here."

"They've got you on cleanup duty, huh?" I don't know how words are even coming out of my mouth, because my brain just wants to focus on the memory of kissing Max last night.

"Glamorous, I know."

"Things around here look good, though," I say, and mean it.

"Like a different place, right?" We gaze down Jersey Street together. I stand closer to him—but not too close, in case other chasers are watching us—and take in how much has been done in such a small amount of time. The fallen trees are all but gone, the stray shingles and debris have been picked up, and a blue tarp is already covering the gaping hole in the roof of the Good Shepherd.

"Hope you've said your prayers recently," Max says, "'cuz we've all been asked to help out in the House of the Lord after this. From what I hear, the money they raised at the Pig & Spit last night bought the supplies the Blisters and Torbros need to clean up their hallowed ground. Though, personally, I'm worried that if they put me on the job, I might burst into flames the minute I step over the threshold."

"Why, what have you done that's been so bad?"

Max grins at me. "The Max Vaughn files are sealed, but I can tell you right now, it's not as bad as what you're probably thinking."

"I'm picturing you helping lost kittens find their way home."

"Okay," he says, "it's a *little* worse than that."

"Let's get over to the church, then," I say. "I'll keep the fire extinguisher close."

20

I definitely don't expect to see Ethan when I pull open the heavy wooden doors to the sanctuary. After my conversation with Hallie, I figured he'd be as bad off as she is, holed up at the motel and trying to recover.

But to my surprise, he and Mason are just inside the door, carrying buckets of plaster down the aisle. "Heya, Jane!" Ethan says, catching sight of me. "I'd wave, but my hands are a little full."

"No worries," I reply, ignoring my urge to run up and ask what in the world went down with Hallie last night. There are just too many people around—not to mention Weather Network cameras.

"Yar, fine day to ye, wench," Mason says by way of greeting. I look at Max, unsure, exactly, how to explain the talk-like-a-pirate thing. Instead, I just shrug.

"They need help in the sanctuary here," Ethan calls, mounting the stairs near the front altar, "but if you get bored with that and want to do some heavy lifting, come to the second floor. The damage is worse there."

"We'll be on the lookout for scallywags in the crow's nest!" Mason says, taking the stairs behind Ethan. "Come up—if ye dare!"

I move to follow them both, but stop when I realize I'm standing on the shredded pages of books. It takes me a second to figure out it's just *one* book. The Good Book. And so many of them were blown to bits in the storm that the entire floor is littered with pages of scripture. I look down and see snippets:

Then Abraham rose from beside his dead wife . . .
Do not be afraid or terrified because of them, for the Lord your God goes with you . . .
After Jesus was born in Bethlehem in Judea . . .
I stretch out my hand against it to cut off its food supply and send famine upon it . . .

Something about walking on the Bible feels wrong. Like picking flowers in a graveyard. "Um, Max, are you seeing what we're stepping on?"

"Totally," says Max. "And I'm legit creeped."

"If it makes you feel better, you could help put the papers in this trash receptacle." A plump woman with flower-patterned gloves—I figure her for a church employee—holds out a plastic bag to me, and I take it. "And, if you wanted, you could send your friend upstairs to help the other men," she says, looking from me to Max.

"Er, okay?" I try to read Max's expression.

"Sure," he says to me. "I'll be with the menfolk doing manly work, and hopefully I'll see you at lunch when you wear a dress and we talk to each other through a curtain."

I snort, but the flowered-glove lady doesn't think it's funny at all. "We appreciate diligent labor," she says. "We're hoping to have services going again by Sunday. Please commit all your efforts here to God."

I'm not sure, but I think that's the Good Shepherd's way of saying work super hard, or else.

With a final wink, Max takes off for the upstairs. The flowered-glove lady leaves, and I begin crumpling thin Bible pages in my hand, one after the other, stuffing them into the garbage bag.

Unfortunately, I don't get very far before my cell phone vibrates in my pocket. I pull it out, and when the caller ID says "Mom," I duck out of the church and hide behind some nearby lilac bushes. I want to be triple sure the Weather Network cameras don't film or record whatever it is that happens next.

"Hi, Janey. How's my girl?"

Of course the one time I find the perfect place to talk privately, she sounds fine—like she wasn't at Larry's until all hours last night. I stare at leaves made translucent by the sun. "I'm okay. What's going on?"

"I FedEx'd you something, and it looks like it went to the wrong place. It's important, so I need the address of where you're staying right now so I can get it rerouted."

My mind is racing. What in the world could it be? "Are you in trouble?" I ask.

"No. There's just some things you need to know."

My heartbeat speeds up. "So just tell me now."

"Janey, give me the address already."

I file through the possibilities of what the FedEx might say. She's lost her job. She's depressed. She's met someone and is getting married.

"Janey," my mom says after a moment, "don't sit there trying to figure this out. Just give me the address."

My hands are shaking. My palms are so slick with sweat, I worry I'm going to drop the phone.

Mom sighs. "I can *hear* you freaking out, you know. The way you're breathing—you sound like you did that day at Dairy Queen when you thought you ate a cricket."

"I—I wasn't expecting a crunch in my ice cream," I say.

"Janey, it was a *cherry*. In a *sundae*."

My head is starting to pound. "Mom, you can't just say you're going to send me something important and then not tell me what it is. Besides, a FedEx is, like, thirty bucks."

"Janey," my mom says. "*Please*." I'm not used to hearing her plead.

"Fine," I relent. "We're at the Palomino Stallion Suites in Clarkstown."

My mom giggles. "That sounds like the name of a strip club."

I smile. "It kinda does, doesn't it?"

"Just don't let any creepy men try to shove one-dollar bills into your panties."

"Mom!"

"I sent your envelope to the Days Inn, but they're going to run it over to you. You'll have it this afternoon."

"We were at the Days Inn in the last town," I say. My smile fades. "You promise me everything is okay?" I ask.

"I promise, baby girl. I promise."

I close my eyes and want for all the world to believe her.

21

I step back onto the lawn of the church and stare at its dark, carved entrance. I don't really feel like going back into the sanctuary and picking up more Bible pages, but I also don't want to go back to the motel and sit around waiting around for my mom's FedEx to arrive.

Just then, Ethan bursts out the front of the church, carrying two empty paint cans. He pulls up short when he sees me. "Hey," he says, "what are you doing out here?"

Ethan's shirt is soaked with sweat, and there's a sprinkling of white plaster in his hair that makes it seem like he's going gray. I want to tell him about Mom's FedEx, but I'm not sure this is the best time.

"Nothing," I say. "I'm just taking a quick break before I go back inside to do more cleaning."

Ethan sets down the paint cans and wipes his forehead with his right forearm. "Never play poker," he says, pulling a bottle of water from his back pocket and taking a swig. "You're an easy mark."

"What?"

"You get this *V* just above your eyebrows. It's a sign you're bothered by something." He caps the bottle. "Care to share?"

I want to rub out the *V* with my palm, but I don't. Instead, I stare at him and wonder how we got here, with him grilling me for every detail in my life but never giving anything up himself.

"Maybe you should go first," I say, flashing back to my fight with Hallie. "Maybe you should tell me about how you drink now. Or about how you hooked up with Hallie. Are you throwing 'em back because she can drink, so you figure you might as well too?"

Ethan pales. "Excuse me?"

"You heard me."

"No. Who told you that?"

"Hallie. Straight from the horse's mouth. You got wasted with her, then hooked up."

Ethan grabs my arm and pulls me away from the church door. We end up back at the lilac bushes where I'd just taken the call from Mom. "If you're talking about last night at the Pig & Spit," Ethan says, his voice low, "then, yes, I had a couple beers. And yes, Hallie and I . . . got close. But it's none—and I mean *none*—of your business, Jane. You hear me?"

"How is it not my business?" I ask, trying to control the tremble in my voice. "You're drinking now too, Einstein. Just like Mom. Don't you get it?"

"Because I had two beers at the Pig & Spit? Now I have a problem?"

"Hallie said you were wasted."

"Two beers is a lot for me. Was I tipsy? Yeah. Does that mean I'm an alcoholic? No way. I'm careful about this stuff, Jane. You of all people should know that."

"You still hooked up with Hallie."

"Not because I was wasted. I *like* Hallie. I've liked her for a long time, actually. The moment was right, and I made my move. And not that you need to know *any* of this, but she called me on my cell a few minutes ago, and we talked. We're going to try things out for real. See where they might head."

Somehow, this makes me more angry, not less. The idea of Hallie and Ethan as an item feels like I'm getting shoved to the back burner so Ethan can focus on his love life. Not that I need tons of attention—I don't. But I could use a hand figuring out what to do about Mom. Which means more than just leaving her to fend for herself back in Minnesota, thank you very much.

"Dammit, Jane," Ethan says, squeezing the bridge of his nose, "I don't understand what's gotten into you. You're running around making a big deal out of things that aren't, and the things that *are* a big deal you just seem to ignore."

"Like what?" I snap.

"Going to Al-Anon. Living with me. Seeing a counselor."

More lists. Inside, the black hole opens again, whispering to me that if Ethan can cut our mom off for not doing what he wants, he'll cut me off, too. Like Mom said he would. He and Hallie will ride off into the sunset together, abandoning me in some run-down motel room.

"She's sending me a FedEx, you know," I say. "I want to see what's inside before I go doing anything super dramatic."

"A FedEx? Really? You're going to put your life on hold for that?"

"You say that like you already know what's inside."

"I do," Ethan says, gazing at the bright sky above us, like the package is there and he can already see it. "It's a bunch of empty promises."

"No!" I cry, frustration making my head hurt. "That's not true. She could write to say she got the Honda fixed. Or come clean about where all the money's going. Or . . ." I let the words die on my lips. I can tell from the look on Ethan's face I shouldn't have said any of that.

"You think the money's going somewhere besides booze?" There's a note in his voice that actually sounds like alarm.

"No," I say, waving the question away. "I just meant—"

Ethan grabs my hands. "*Don't lie to me.* Where is the money going?"

My anger vanishes. All that's left is cold fear.

"I don't know," I whisper. At least that much is true. "I don't know where the money's going. But it's more than ever. She'd have to be drinking *so* much for all of it to disappear like that."

Ethan lets go of my hands. "She's into something worse, then? Meth? Oxy?"

I shake my head, wanting the idea to fly out of my brain,

like a dog trying to shake off water after a bath. I don't know the answer.

I don't *want* to know the answer.

"Aw, Jesus, Jane," Ethan says. I stare at the grass, mottled with sunlight and shade. "All this after what happened to Uncle Pete. I don't get it. You'd think that would have been a *warning*."

It wasn't a warning as much as a punishment, I think. My mom used to have Pete over for dinner when Ethan and I were little—but she told him never to come back after he broke into our apartment and stole our DVD player, hawking it for drug money. That was a few years ago, and up until he died, she'd just shake her head when she got a collect call from him. "I'm too busy trying to get by my damn self," she'd say, slamming the receiver down. "I don't have time to get taken advantage of."

When she got the news he'd passed—that he'd *frozen,* shrunken and cold in the back of his car, his frostbitten body black and decaying—she sat on the couch for an entire day sipping whiskey. It was Pete's favorite, she said, like she was drinking it in his memory, straight out of the bottle.

After that, she blacked out so hard, she was in bed for nineteen hours straight. It was the first time I'd shaken my mom and wondered if she was dead. I remember the stabbing fear I'd felt as I'd gripped her shoulder and rolled her onto her side. My vision narrowed into two tiny pinpricks, focused on her face, pale and greasy and tinged with green. When she groaned and pushed me away, I burst into tears.

"What if I leave Mom and she dies like Uncle Pete?" I mumble the question, almost asking myself.

"Mom's going to do what Mom's going to do. Same as Pete."

"But Mom could have *helped* him."

Ethan shakes his head. "Uncle Pete didn't want help. He probably just wanted money. Or another chance to steal stuff for drug money. I don't know, but I'm guessing that if he was clean and needed food or shelter, he could have found it. It's not always easy to get those things when you're homeless, but I'll tell you, it's a lot harder when you're not *sober*."

We're quiet for a few minutes until Ethan clears his throat. "I'm sure to you the Pete stuff makes it seem like Mom might meet the same end. It's hard to think about, I know, but if she decides to go down that road, you can't stop her." His straight-lined jaw flexes—like he's chewing on his next words, softening them before they come out. "Jane, it's going to kill me if you go back there. I'm not saying that to make you feel guilty. If there's guilt here, it's mine. For leaving you with her. But, cripes. Think about this. Mom's not just losing one war, she's probably starting a second with a new drug. And she's about to take you down into the trenches with her."

His face is lined with pain, and in that second, I wish I could make all Ethan's hurt go away. The words *I'll stay* are right there on the tip of my tongue.

I forgive you.

I'll stay.

Until I remember that there's a good chance I wouldn't be here if Ethan hadn't left Mom and me in the first place. Maybe things would have turned out differently if he'd stuck around. It's possible Mom wouldn't be this bad off if she'd just had a little more help. Like Uncle Pete, who, for all we know, could have been trying to get his life back together and we just ignored him.

Besides, what if *I* fall and need help getting back on *my* feet? Would Ethan just leave me, too? Not that I'm looking to get hooked on drugs, but life can get tough in a thousand other ways, and you need people who will stick by you. Even if I move down here, I'm just not sure Ethan will be there for me.

"I just—I should probably get back to work," I say.

Ethan's face crumples, and my heart constricts. He's really trying to help me. But then he takes a breath and nods, like whatever I'm going to do, I'm going to do and he can't be bothered with it. "Fine by me," he says.

We stand there for a moment until Ethan walks back to the paint cans by the church's front door. He picks them up like they weigh a thousand pounds. I watch him carry them to the Dumpster halfway down the block. When he chucks them in, I step out from behind the lilac bush and head in the opposite direction.

22

Thank God I have my camera with me, I think, as I walk down Jersey Street. Nothing sounds as good as putting my lens between me and the world for a while. I'm sick of seeing things without a filter.

I'm headed south, toward where we found Danny. There's no sidewalk, so I walk against the traffic, not that there's much of it. A baby-blue pickup truck grinds by, and the driver lifts his hand off the steering wheel as he passes. I wave back.

Once I cross the tracks, the cars are practically nonexistent, save for the rusted ones on blocks behind the pole barns and outbuildings. I hear a dog bark and the high-pitched whirr of a cicada, but other than that, it's quiet.

About a half block up, I spot an ancient chain-link fence and, just beyond it, cracked blacktop and a leaning basketball hoop. As I get closer, I see that what was once a paved and painted court has been damaged from years of neglect—not from the recent storm. I snap a few photos of the threadbare basketball net and the shattered backboard before I note two peeling park benches in the distance. There's someone sitting on one of them.

I'm about to turn and leave when the person stands and, to my surprise, calls my name. I squint into the sun and try to make out who it is. It's not until he's much closer that I realize—it's Victor.

His black hair is tucked under a Nebraska Huskers baseball cap, and he's wearing aviator sunglasses. He's pale like Hallie, and I'm going to guess more than a little hungover like her, too.

"I figured it was you taking pictures," he says by way of greeting.

"I'm a little bit tired of cleanup patrol in town," I lie, "so I thought I'd take a break and come down here."

Victor nods and watches the sky for a second. I wrestle with what to say, since I'm not exactly sure how much of last night he remembers. "I guess they're predicting more big storms tomorrow," he offers after a bit. "South of here, though. Oklahoma."

"How do you feel about that?" I ask, realizing too late I sound like a lame therapist. He turns to me and I can see my reflection in his sunglasses.

"I think you know how I feel."

Obviously he remembers a *lot* about last night.

"If you're worried I'm going to tell anyone what you said—"

His mouth quirks, making his scar jump. "Shit. What I slurred to you is the worst-kept secret in the chasing world.

Everybody knows I lost it last year. Everybody knows I'm holding my dick in my hand. They just don't talk about it to my face."

Unsure of how to respond, I watch heat waves shimmer above the blacktop.

"What you did last night was nice," Victor says after a second. "Helping me. Listening to me. In case I forget to say it later, I'll say it now: thanks."

The heat waves look like water. A mirage. "Except what will you do?" I ask. "The way you painted it, if you chase, you're screwed. If you don't chase, the team is screwed."

"Hell of a dilemma, isn't it?" Victor's gaze is back on me. "Sorry if you told me last night what *you'd* do. I don't remember."

The mirage is widening, glimmering like a lake. I watch it, thinking the answer is so obvious in Victor's case. *Leave. Live your life. The Torbros will be fine.*

The same thing I'd do in my own life if it didn't mean everything would come crashing down on my mom. I can't set myself free if it means she might die. I flash back to the Bible pages I cleaned up, of how they all said the opposite through the story of Jesus. He died so you might live. I live so my mom might not die. Amen and amen.

"I keep going over the options," Victor says, when I don't speak. "And maybe it's not as bad as I think."

"How?"

"Let's say, for example, that I leave the team and we lose the bet. The terms of the bet are that Alex gets Polly's schematics.

Even with blueprints, it's going to take him at least a month to build a prototype of her. The Blisters will be lucky if they get her out in the field this season. Even if they do, there's no guarantee she'll actually get data. In that time, I could build something else. I'm not a one-trick pony."

"But the funding—it's all based off Polly," I say.

"And we're still pulling numbers from her. *We* have the working machine, not the Blisters. If I had to, I could get Mason up to speed on her for the rest of this season. It wouldn't be a picnic, but it'd be doable. So, to me, Polly's the easy part."

"Then what's the hard part?" I ask.

"Stephen. The fact that the side of the van says *Tornado Brothers*. The fact that Stephen thinks I should just . . . get over this."

I try to stop my brain from connecting more dots between me and Victor, but I can't. The way I bend and twist and adjust so my mom can have an easier time of it—it's the same way Victor's putting Stephen's life ahead of his own.

"Truth is," Victor says, "I got into this thinking I could protect Stephen. But if I don't get out of the field, I'm afraid I'm going to really hurt someone. Really fuck up in a way I can't take back. Or run from."

"So, Stephen should understand that, right?"

"Maybe. Probably. But the big question is, will I still walk away if he doesn't?"

My throat is suddenly on fire. I swallow a few times to cool it down.

"You okay?" Victor asks.

I stare at him. It's the same. His situation and mine.

"Look," Victor says, pulling off his sunglasses and gazing at me with his dark eyes, "I didn't mean to get all heavy with this stuff. Ethan's mentioned some shit about your mom, drinking and whatnot, and I'm sorry if I put you on the spot last night. You acted like a real pro, though, and I appreciate it."

"Forget about that," I say. "What about you? What will you *do*?"

Victor smiles. "Leave. Stephen might never understand it. I'm his big brother, after all. The one who's supposed to be looking out for him, the one who's supposed to know what's best. Except that's not true anymore. He's making too many excuses for me, and he just doesn't need me. He's got a whole chase team behind him now. If I let him down, I guess I feel like I could live with his disappointment a lot easier than I could live with physically hurting someone. Or even killing someone."

Above us, a cluster of starlings darts across the sky. "When?" I ask after the birds have fluttered into the distance. "When will you take off?"

"I don't know. It's probably like a Band-Aid—better to rip it off and be done with it. I just have to talk to Stephen first. So, if you would, don't go telling anyone about this until I have a chance to talk with him."

"Sure. Of course."

My cell buzzes, and I pull it out. It's a text from Max. **Where r u? Can I c u later?**

"Pressing business?" Victor asks.

"No. Maybe. I don't know."

Victor smirks. "Is it the Backstreet Boy I saw you dancing with last night? The one that helped Danny?"

I look at him. "Maybe?"

Victor actually laughs. "I'll leave you to it, then," he says, taking a few steps toward the road. "But, in case you're wondering, I guess everyone's meeting for dinner tonight at Applebee's. Something about needing salads and Cokes after last night." He glances at my phone. "If you don't make it for . . . whatever reason, I'll tell them you weren't feeling well. Deal?"

I smile. "Deal. And thanks."

Victor gives me one last nod, then starts up the street.

23

My motel room is shadowy in the late afternoon, but I haven't turned on any lights. I'm sitting in the semidarkness on the edge of my bed, which is the same position I've been in since I opened my door and saw the FedEx had been slid under the crack. Waiting for me.

I glance down at my phone when a text from Max lights up the screen. Alex is finally off my bak. How bout I come pick u up? We can go 2 barn agn.

My eyes flick from the phone to the FedEx, and my stomach knots all over again. Do I even want to know what it says?

I need to be like Victor, I think. Just rip it open and get it over with. And then, no matter what it says, stop living my life for my mom.

Easier said than done, of course. And there's always Ethan to consider. He says he wants me to come live with him, but he could always change his mind. Leave me again when I inevitably can't be the perfect sister he wants me to be. Run off and live his new, perfect life with Hallie. And then I'd really be screwed.

Another of my mom's expressions jumps into my head. *Piss or get off the pot, Janey.*

I either need to face this FedEx or just toss it in the trash.

I tell myself I'll have an easier time reading it if I reward myself with seeing Max after it's over. **I'm in rm 119**, I text Max. **Say 15 min?**

His reply is immediate. **Cool c u then.**

I glance at the clock: 7:46. I have until 8:01 to read this. The rest of the Torbros are all still at Applebee's, so there's no way I'm going to get interrupted.

I just need to do it already.

I turn the envelope over and over in my hands. Down the hall a door slams. The air conditioner's hum fills the room.

"Come on," I say out loud. "You can do this."

I rip open the envelope and pull out a single sheet of paper. It's a handwritten note from my mom, scrawled on letterhead from work.

Dear Janey,

I've started this note a thousand times and each time is worse than the last. So I'm just going to cut to the chase. I am going to rehab. Starting right away. I'll be gone for a while at the White Pine Recovery Center up near Duluth. Would you believe the girls at the clinic raised the $500

it cost to send me there? I was too scared to tell you myself
on the phone, so that's why I sent you this letter. I figured
hearing your voice would make me think I didn't need to
stop drinking. Because then I'd talk myself into believing
you'd take care of me. But you're not here. So I'm taking off
for a while. Okay? I'll be out in a few weeks. I love you,

Mom

I look up from the note, but I don't see the motel room. My mind is a thousand miles away in Duluth, where my mom is getting help.

I can practically smell the hallways—a blend of bleach and antiseptic. I can feel the lumpy, hard bed she'll sleep in, and my hands tremble just slightly, like my mom's do when I know she's aching for a drink. She won't have one, though, because she'll be getting help instead.

I clutch the note to my chest. Ethan was wrong! What was in the FedEx matters more than he could know. It changes everything!

If I could dance, I'd shake what I've got. Instead, when Max comes to the door, I throw my arms around him and press my lips against his. We kiss in the open doorway until Max shuts the door with his foot. Then I push him against the closed door and kiss him harder. The touch of his warm lips feels like the perfect way to express the happiness in my heart. *My mom is getting better.*

"Wow," says Max when we finally pull apart. "What was that for?"

"I got some good news," I say, knowing I'm grinning like an idiot.

"Care to share?"

"Come here," I say, pulling him over to the bed. The springs squeak as we sit on the end. I take a breath. "My mom has a problem," I start.

"Only one?"

"One bad one. She has a drinking problem."

Max takes my hand. "I'm sorry. That's no small thing."

"I know. And, it's hard to talk about usually. It's not like I go around telling everyone that. But today I got some good news. She wrote me a note to say she's going into rehab."

Max flashes his trillion-watt smile. "Dude, really? That's huge. Seriously. I'm so glad."

A bubbly laugh erupts from my throat. "I know, right? I'm so happy!"

"I bet it means you'll worry a lot less about her."

I nod. "There's that for sure. I thought I was going to have to leave her. My brother, he of course knows how my mom can be, and he invited me to come live with him after the chase season wraps. But now I don't have to. I can go back to Minnesota."

I can't believe how much I'm telling Max. But I don't even care. I let the words come, unbidden, because it's okay. Things are going to turn out just fine.

Max's smile falters. "Your mom ever do rehab before?"

"Once, yeah. But it was a while ago, and my brother practically blackmailed her into doing it. This time is way different.

My best friend, Cat? She almost died because of my mom. So my mom knows it has to stick."

"Okay," Max says, but his expression is clouded.

"What? Why do you look like that?"

"Like what?"

"Like you don't believe what I'm telling you," I say. I walk to the dresser where the note's lying, facedown. "You want to read what she said?"

"No," Max says, "no, I totally believe your mom's giving this an honest go. It's you I'm worried about."

"Me? Why?"

Max pats the flowered bedspread, and I sit down beside him again. "Look. My dad's brother, my uncle Frank? He's an alcoholic too. And what he went through to get sober was no picnic. But his wife, my aunt Betty—some days we were more worried about her than Frank."

"What do you mean?"

"Like, there'd be these times Uncle Frank would get clean but then just fall into his old habits again because she made it so easy. Not on purpose, but she didn't know what else to do. She'd call in to work for him, make sure everything around the house was taken care of, make excuses when he got loaded at family functions.

"So this last time my uncle Frank comes out of rehab and— *bam*. Betty's not there. She left. She went to her sister's and stayed there for six months. And she got help too, you know? She got counseling and all sorts of stuff so she wouldn't be

Frank's crutch if—or when—he started going off the wagon. Turns out Betty needed just as much help as he did."

I sit up straighter. "So, what? You're telling me I need to go to a facility too?"

"Hey, easy," Max says. "I'm not trying to shit on your parade. I'm just telling you this stuff is hard. And lots of times the people closest to alcoholics, they need help as well. It's not a bad thing."

There's a pinprick of pain at the base of my neck that I think might flower into a migraine at any second. Why is Max telling me about his aunt Betty like my situation is the same? I get that life with an alcoholic is no picnic. Lord knows I understand that. But the situation with his aunt and uncle isn't *my* situation—not by a long shot.

"Hey," Max says, putting his hand on my cheek, "I'm sorry. I'm not trying to make this harder on you. It's good news about your mom going to rehab. For sure. Let's just focus on that for now."

He kisses me gently. I let his soft breath and strong arms erase all the tension between us. "You still want to go to the barn?" he asks after a moment. "It's a perfect night for sitting in the hayloft. Which, I know, is quite a date proposal. There's a girl out there eating lobster at a sit-down restaurant who's green with envy."

I smile. "I do, I really do, but it's probably too far. I should stick closer and try to find Ethan tonight before it gets too late. He needs to know about my mom's note too."

Max takes a breath. "Cool. So we'll do something nearby. My motel has an outdoor pool. Most of the Blisters are down the road at a bar, so it's not like they'll see us if we go stick our toes in the shallow end."

I hesitate. Now that I've told Max about my mom, I feel closer to him than ever—not farther away, like I thought I would. But still, there's a sharp uneasiness inside me. Should I really spend any more time with him? Maybe it'll be tomorrow, maybe it'll be the day after, but one day the Blisters will pack their vans and leave. Max will be gone. The barn, dancing at the Pig & Spit, the way his lips taste—it will vanish. All of it.

Because that's what happens. Eventually, someone has to leave.

So add tonight to the pile of memories, I tell myself, *then sweep it away like dust. Ashes to ashes, Max to Max.*

"All right," I say. I take his hand and squeeze it. "Let's do this."

We step outside into the rustling summer night. The surprised face of the man in the moon reflects on every car in the parking lot. "Is the moon this big everywhere, or is it just the plains?" I ask, tilting my head back.

"I think it's even bigger in Texas. Supposedly everything's enormous there. Their twisters get to be EF-11s."

I giggle as we reach the end of the parking lot and walk past Happy's, making our way along the road. A few cars and trucks rumble past underneath the glare of the orange streetlights, but for the most part, everything is quiet. We get to Max's motel—the C'mon Inn—and walk around the side to the pool. The filter hums as Max pulls up two lounge chairs.

We lie side by side, both of us staring at the stars, which are sparse and pale in the moon's white light.

"So how do you think your team liked Patchy Falls?" Max asks, reaching out and taking my hand, connecting us over the plastic armrests. "You think they got themselves in front of the Weather Network enough?"

"It's been good," I reply, trying to ignore the way Max's thumb is stroking my palm. "I mean, who knows what the network will air when it comes down to it, but they definitely have footage of us helping clean up the town. And that's awesome."

"That douche Victor sure didn't make it easy on you guys, did he?"

I sit up, disconnecting us. "No, it's not like that. There was an accident last year, and Victor got kind of messed up over it. You didn't hear?"

Max shakes his head.

"The Torbros got caught in a storm," I explain. "Victor almost died, and that's how he got that scar on his face. Probably now he has something like post-traumatic stress syndrome, but some of the chasers just think he's a coward."

"Still, the way he ran away from Danny like that . . ."

"I know," I agree. "It was bad. And Victor knows it too. He doesn't want to put anyone else in danger, which is why he's leaving the team really soo—" I clap my hand over my mouth, horrified. Did I really just blab Victor's exodus to Max?

Max pulls my hand gently away from my mouth. His fingers

are warm. "It's okay," he says. "If you're worried I'm going to tell anyone, I'm not."

"*No one* can find out before Stephen. Victor still has to talk to him."

"It's cool. Really." Max pulls me closer to him. He runs a finger along my eyebrow, down my cheek, all the way to my neck. Sparklers ignite everywhere he touches me. "I won't say anything," he whispers. His lips are close to mine, then *on* mine, and he's pulling me on top of him so we're both in the same lounge chair.

Thigh on thigh, chest on chest, we're so close, there's not even night between us. My heart's thumping so hard, I wonder if he can feel it through our T-shirts. His hands are on my back, in my hair, on my hips. His fingers move like I'm Braille, like he's trying to read me just by touching me.

He kisses me and our breath tangles so it's impossible to tell whose air is whose. I let my lungs fill with the taste and smell of him. Behind my closed eyes I can picture his cells going deep into my lungs where they mix with my blood—with my tissue.

That's when I roll off him and stand. I told myself this was nothing, but here I am, fantasizing about being *filled* with him, for crying out loud. Like he's this fount of intoxication and I'm just . . . drinking from it. How can you leave someone if you let them this deep inside you?

It's so much harder that way. Messy. Complicated. No Band-Aids.

So this ends. *Now.*

"I have to go," I say, backing away from the lounge chairs. "I'm sorry."

"What?" Max says, sitting up. His dark eyebrows are knotted together. "What is it?"

"Nothing," I stammer. I pull open the pool gate. "Just forget it. I'll see you later."

Before he can scheme or plan or try to fix this or try to change my mind, I sprint away. It's better like this, I tell myself. I ignore the ache in my heart and the face of the man in the moon who's looking at me like *wtf*?

It was never going to work out. Someone had to go. I just did it before he could, because I know how it feels to be the one left behind. You pick up the pieces while the other person starts a brand-new happy life without you. No way was I going to let that happen to me again. Not if I could help it.

My chest is heaving as I slide the key into my door. I focus on the burning in my lungs, trying to block out the still-lingering feeling of Max on my skin and lips. I force myself to think about the FedEx instead.

I'm ready to find Ethan. To show him Mom's note. To forget Maximilian Adam Whittaker Vaughn altogether.

24

Ethan opens the door, his forehead drawn in confusion. "What's going on? Why are you pounding on my door like an ape?"

"This!" I say, stepping into the room. He closes the door, and I place the stationery into his hand. "You said the FedEx wouldn't matter, but it does. You *gotta* read it."

I study his face as he scans the note. But there's nothing—not a smile, not a nod. He hands the paper back to me, his chiseled face even stonier.

"Good for her," he says.

The air-conditioned motel room is suddenly freezing. "That's it?"

Ethan rubs the bridge of his nose. "Look, Jane. We both know Mom's done this before. It didn't stick. So, fine. She's in rehab again. Awesome. But I'm not going to start waving the victory flag just yet. Let's see where she is in three months, not three weeks."

I can hardly believe this. "Are you serious? Are you actually one hundred percent for real right now?"

Ethan walks over to the bed and closes his laptop, where he'd been looking at weather maps. The lid shuts with a soft click. "I don't know what you want me to say. You want me to tell you it's awesome? That everything's different? That you should totally go back to Minnesota now and live with her?"

"That'd be a nice start."

"Based on what?" Ethan asks, his eyes blazing. "Based on a piece of paper you brought into my motel room? Jesus, Jane. Don't you know you can't trust her? For all we know, she could be in Arizona right now. There's no guarantee at all she's at this White Pine place."

"Of course she's there!"

Ethan rolls his eyes. "Sure. Okay. But here's another thing. If she's only getting treated for alcohol at White Pine and she's crossed over into some other drug, then she's going to crash and burn worse than the Hindenburg."

"The what?"

"This blimp the Germans made that—oh, never mind. Look, will you just listen to me, I mean really listen to me, if I tell you something important?"

"What?" I fold my arms like I can hardly be bothered, but the truth is he has my total attention.

"I need you to hear me when I tell you I'm sorry I left you with Mom when you were little. I had to get out. And now I know that anything I say about her is colored against *that choice*. That I left. I'm the one who walked out."

That pretty much sums it up, I want to say, but I don't.

"But I really didn't go far. I mean, look at me. I chase tornadoes. I chase *chaos,* because it's what I know. It's what I'm comfortable with. I left home, but I still need a little bit of Mom around, don't I?"

I stare at him.

"My point is," he continues, "you can get comfortable with anything. I think you and I are both pretty comfortable with chaos. The difference is, I left Minnesota and found a different form of it. A healthier form, as long as I don't get hit by tornadic projectiles. And you need to leave Minnesota, too. Whether Mom goes to rehab or not, you need to focus on *you* for a while."

"But if she's better—"

"It's not about her. If she's better, then awesome. Then she's better. She'll be fine. And if she's worse, then you've protected yourself by not getting back into the thick of it."

I shift my weight, still unsure. I thought Mom going to rehab changed everything, and now Ethan is saying it doesn't change *anything.* Which might have been the same thing that Max was trying to say. Except, how can that be?

"Look," Ethan says gently, "I'm running out of ways to say that you need to start thinking about *you.* But it's true. And the other thing that's true is that Mom's 'rehab' might feel like a big deal to you tonight, but it's only going to be big when she's sober. So think on that, okay? Will you just promise me you'll sleep on it and not buy a plane ticket back to Minnesota right away?"

Ethan looks so tired and earnest that I have to nod. "All right, then," he says. "We're leaving Patchy Falls in the morning. Get some rest. We'll need to be on the road by eight, so make sure you're packed and ready by then."

I leave him, my heart jumbled like the pieces of the Good Shepherd's stained glass. If nothing else, Ethan is right about one thing: I don't have to figure it all out tonight.

25

The next morning when I enter the breakfast room, I'm surprised to see that Alex Atkins and a cameraman are already there.

"You can just put everything on our servers," Alex is saying to Stephen, who looks like he would haul off and punch Alex in the face if the cameras weren't right there. Behind Stephen, Victor and Ethan stand near a table cluttered with laptops and power cords. Mason and Hallie are frozen at the buffet, watching the conversation go down. "I mean, we all figured Victor would be running for the hills eventually. But so soon?"

My heart soars. Victor must have said something last night to Stephen about quitting.

"Enough, Alex," Stephen growls. "You're getting what you want. Now shut up about it."

Victor puts a hand on his brother's shoulder. "Dude," he says. "Don't let him get to you. It was just a matter of time—"

"No it wasn't!" Stephen spins around and glares at his brother. "You do *not* have to stand there and let this happen. You are *fine*. This is all in your head, and if you could just realize that, you'd keep us from losing Polly! She's our one advantage in this field!"

Victor shakes his head. "It's not that simple, Steve. I'm a liability. And besides, I can build more instrumentation if I just—"

"If you stay, we keep priority over the instrumentation we have now!"

Victor swallows visibly. His scar moves up and down. "I'm not trying to piss you off. But I'm not cut out for chasing. I never have been. This is your dream, man. For a while there I let it be mine, because I thought you needed me. And that's just not true anymore."

Behind his beard, Stephen's face falls. "But I do need you. We're the Tornado Brothers. I've never chased without you, Vic. I mean, what the hell? How are we supposed to do this?"

"Come on. Really? The leader of this group is you. Always has been. You know that."

"Perhaps, but you're the only one who really knows how to extract the right data from Polly."

"I think I can get Mason up to speed. A few phone calls, e-mail him a few documents. Hell, I can always meet you on the road if you're really struggling with her."

"No," Stephen rumbles. "It's bigger than that. What you're doing is effectively putting an end to the Tornado Brothers. To our team."

Victor cocks a dark eyebrow. "Last time I checked, you still had a hell of a group with you."

Alex takes a step forward. "As touching as all this is, and as much as I'd love to stick around and watch the soap opera unfold, I need to go. So I'll expect the schematics for Polly within a week. Text me when they're ready, and we'll give you directions for posting them to our shared space."

"Aw, screw that," Mason says, striding over from the buffet. "Steve, tell this guy to shove his Doppler up his ass. We don't have to honor that bet."

Stephen smiles sadly. "Losing to this guy sucks. I know. But we shook on it, and our word's our word."

Mason sticks his finger in Alex's face. "This be not done, bilge rat," he says, leering with his best pirate face. "We'll give ye no quarter for the rest of the season."

"Freak," Alex mutters, his little body twitching in disdain. He turns to leave, but as he does, he catches sight of me. "Ah, the intern! The girl I must thank for her information. How are you?"

I struggle to process Alex's words. What information does he mean? "Excuse me?"

"Telling Max what you did gave us a head start on Victor's plans. Very nice of you."

I look over at Ethan, whose eyes have gone round. Stephen glares at me, then starts punching buttons on his laptop.

A whip cracks over my heart, sending pain searing through my chest. I realize Alex is saying that *he* broke the news of Victor's departure to Stephen. Victor didn't even get to tell his own brother the news—because of me. Because Max told Alex what I shared with him last night.

I swallow down nausea. *Don't throw up on camera,* is all I can think. "That can't be. Max would never say anything."

Alex winks at me. "Wouldn't he, now?"

He would if he was angry enough, I think. *If he was pissed off about the way you ran away from him.*

My mouth is partway open, and I can't seem to close it.

"Well, this has been fun," Alex says. "I look forward to getting to know Polly much better."

The minute he's left the room, I rush Victor. "I didn't mean to say anything," I wheeze, trying to catch my breath since suddenly it feels like I just ran a marathon. "It was an accident."

Stephen's head snaps up. "Victor confided his plans to you, and you blabbed them to a Twister Blister. That's information that should have stayed in our group. You should have used discretion!"

"Hey, easy there, bro," Victor says. "Lay off. Ultimately all this is my choice, my fuckup—not Jane's."

Stephen takes a breath. "This can all still go away. If you'd just stay *on*—"

Victor holds up his hands. "No, man. I'm done. I'm sorry, but I'm done."

"So that's it?" Stephen asks quietly.

Victor nods. "That's it."

"What about today's chase?"

"We're headed south, looks like, and that's the direction I

need to go in anyway if I want to get back to the university. I'll bite my fingernails for one more chase if it gets me closer to Norman. Then I can get a rental car home."

"You really going back to the lab then?"

"For now, yeah," Victor says. "To start, I can dig into the data Polly's already pulled. That way we don't have to wait until there's a break in the weather to run analytics. And after that, I can start prototyping some new inventions."

Stephen smooths down his beard. From behind him, Ethan's eyes find mine, sharp enough to bore holes into my skull. The weight of his anger—his disappointment—crushes me.

"From now on, there's to be *no* fraternizing with the Twister Blisters or any other chasing team," Stephen says to me. "Do I make myself clear?"

I nod.

"Fine. We're leaving Patchy Falls and heading south in twenty minutes. Everyone be ready."

He throws a power cord on the table as he strides out of the room. I'm still standing there, trembling. I try not to lose it, but the room goes blurry anyway.

"Jesus," Victor says, standing next to me, "I hate it when girls cry." He hands me a crumpled napkin from his pocket and I wipe my face. "Look, I'm not mad. I'm kind of relieved, actually." I stare at the floor, unsure of what to say.

"Everything's going to be fine," Victor continues, "though I'm going to guess the rest of the team needs time to cool off. It's a tough break for them. So give 'em a few days, and things will be okay again. But don't worry. This isn't your fault. It's mine. And you couldn't know Max was going to say anything. I'm sure he seemed trustworthy."

You have no idea, I think.

Victor reaches out awkwardly and pats my back—once, twice. Sort of like he's not used to touching other people.

"Thanks," I sniff. When my eyes are dry, I begin the long walk of shame back to my room to get my bag.

No one even pretends to look up as I go.

I slink deeper into my seat and stare out the van's window. A coal train rumbles across nearby tracks, shaking our vehicle. In spite of all the noise, I swear the silence is still deafening. At least in my direction, anyway. No one's said a word to me since breakfast.

To make matters worse, I got a text from Max. **R we ok? U left in a hurry lst nite.**

I wanted to throw the phone across the seats when I read it. *No, we are not okay,* I think. *Not after what you did. Where do you get off?* I fight the urge to text back the question. He's not worth it.

I shove my phone into a bag underneath the seat and don't take it out again until we've stopped for lunch.

"Good thing the storms look like they're breaking farther north and east," Ethan says to Mason as we file inside a TGI Friday's rip-off called—no kidding—Thursday's. "Not sure we could have made it all the way down to Lawton before dark."

"But it'll be bad if they move too far into Missouri," Mason says. "More trees and hills there. Makes the chase a lot harder."

The roar of traffic along the highway behind us is suddenly replaced by the blare of Top Forty music inside the purple-and-white-striped restaurant. A hostess wearing a black shirt and yellow suspenders chews on a hunk of gum.

"Six?" she asks. Her eyes are ringed in dark makeup.

"Hi, yes," Hallie says, and we're led to a table. I sit next to Mason, who at least doesn't scoot his chair over to get farther away from me.

"Hey, everyone," our waitress says. "I'm Elise. I'll be taking care of you today." She smiles, and her round face is adorable under a pixie haircut. Beside me, Mason stiffens. His gaze is fixed on Elise's suspenders. He looks like he might pass out. Following his eyes, I spot a *Star Trek* pin next to a *Star Wars* Wookie.

No. Way. Elise is a sci-fi geek.

"What can I get you to drink?" Elise asks. Everyone gives their order, except Mason, who seems to be on the verge of a heart attack.

"Ch—Co—ke . . ."

Elise's brow furrows. "Cherry Coke?" It's all Mason can do to nod.

"Be right back," Elise says. As she turns away, the whole table launches into more weather talk, except for Mason. He's gone totally quiet. When Elise comes back to take our order, Mason barely gets out "baby back ribs."

The food arrives, we eat, and still Mason hasn't said a word. Unfortunately, no one seems to have noticed Mason's possible geek soul mate has served us lunch—except me.

Before the meal is over and Elise can bring us the check, I flag her down. "Excuse me, can I get another Diet Coke?" I'm trying to think of any excuse for her to talk to Mason, who's staring at her like she's Princess Leia come to life. "I'm, uh, totally parched from all the tornado chasing we did this week," I continue. "We were on this storm up in Nebraska, then we stayed in the town it hit to clean up after it did some damage." I know I sound awkward and totally lame, but for crying out loud, she's wearing a Wookie pin.

Elise is too sweet to ignore all my blabber. "Oh, so y'all are tornado chasers?"

"Yeah," I say, nodding. "Mason here is an actual scientist—he could tell you more about the important weather stuff. I'm just tagging along to take pictures."

The whole table has gone quiet, staring at me. They're wondering what in the hell I'm talking about. Except Hallie. She suddenly gets it.

"Yeah. Mason was the star of the day," she says. "Probably we should get a dessert for him. Mason, you feel like a brownie sundae or something?"

Mason turns six shades of scarlet. And then, somehow, he taps into a hidden reservoir of suave. "Sure," he says, finally lifting his eyes to Elise. "I'd love a brownie sundae."

Elise smiles at him. "Nuts and a cherry?"

He nods. "The works." Before she can go, he asks, "You a *Star Wars* fan?"

She looks confused for a second, then remembers. "Oh, the pin. Right? Well, yeah. My girlfriends all make fun of me for it, but I don't care. I suppose I'm a joke to them, watching *Star Wars* and reading comics and watching all these sci-fi shows. Last year I went to that big comic convention in California? Comic-Con? They laughed at me for weeks."

I think Mason's heart might actually come thudding out of his chest. "I—I was there!" he says.

Elise's eyes go round. "Really? No one around here ever knows what Comic-Con is. And you were *there*?"

Mason smiles. I can tell he wants to erupt into the same stories he's told all of us about it, and I say a silent prayer he doesn't. *Be chill, Mason,* I think. *Be totally chill.*

"Are you on Facewars? I'm JangoFett25."

Facewars is like Facebook, but for *Star Wars* nerds.

"Oh, totally," Elise says. "I'm Tarfful-Warrior."

"I'd—I'd love to talk to you more," Mason says. "Can I direct message you?"

Elise glances around the table. The conversation's suddenly taken a personal turn in front of all of us. I don't envy her one bit, and at the same time, I want to blurt out how Mason is a really good guy and she should *definitely* get to know him. And that if they started dating, he'd only be a few hours away at the University of Oklahoma—at least when he wasn't chasing. But I stay quiet.

"Sure," she says after a moment. "That would be cool." She pulls out her waitressing notepad and writes her Facewars name on it. She hands it to Mason, who looks like he's been given a room full of Christmas presents early.

Stephen clears his throat. "I'm sorry, but I think we may need to forgo the sundae." He's staring at his smartphone. "A tornado watch has just been issued twenty minutes south of here. Looks like it could be big. We should roll." He hands Elise a credit card and she trots off to process the bill. I'm about to stand, when Mason grabs my arm.

"Thanks," he whispers, his eyes warm. "That was awesome, the way you handled that."

"No problem," I say, relieved that someone is finally talking to me. "Just don't forget to direct message her."

"Not on your life," he says.

We pay the bill, then all but sprint to the van. The clouds to the south are already darkening, turning from deep blue to black.

"Drive like hell," Stephen tells Hallie, and we peel out of the parking lot.

26

Twenty minutes later, the van hits a bump that launches me a few inches out of my seat, despite my safety belt.

"Stay on this road," Ethan tells Hallie. "I know it's not paved, but we need another mile here, then we put Polly out. After we get our readings, we're back onto pavement."

Hallie glances in the rearview at Ethan, and I know what she's thinking: that this is the stupidest thing we've ever done but she can't argue because Stephen's authorized it. We're on a dirt road because we've got a wall cloud to our south and we're trying to get Polly in the perfect position.

"It's going to be fine," Ethan says as we hit another bump. "There's almost no precipitation around this storm. No worries."

Dust rises behind the van, and rocks clink under the carriage.

"Okay," Stephen says after another mile on the road. He looks at the Doppler and then at the GPS. "I think we should be good here."

Hallie pulls over and is barely stopped before Mason and Ethan have leaped out to set up Polly. I stay in the van, not feeling like taking pictures. Victor's in the passenger seat, up front.

"So no photos?" he asks, turning around to face me when the other chasers are out of the van. His voice is casual, though I can see he's got a white-knuckled grip on the sides of his seat.

"No. Not today."

On the other side of the window, wind tears at the few scrubby trees along a nearby fence line. The bright green field dulls as the grasses flatten against the earth. Victor pulls out his iPod and sticks in his earbuds. "No offense," he says to me, "but I gotta distract myself."

I nod. Outside, I hear a yell. A spinning funnel is starting to drop, about a quarter mile away. Ethan's grinning and pointing at Polly, his white shirt stark against the black sky. Hallie throws herself into his arms, and they laugh with the sound of two people in total like with each other.

They've forgotten I even exist.

I look away.

Just then, my phone buzzes in my jacket pocket. I pull it out to see a new text from Cat.

Hey. Wanted to chk in. How r u?

My muscles go limp with relief. I'm beyond ready to stop thinking about the Torbros and talk with Cat. Ignoring the chaos outside, I type back. **Mixed. Bad day w team. Long story. But my mom sent me a lettr ystrday. She's in rehab!** ☺

A minute later, my phone rings. It's Cat. I glance at Victor, who's got his iPod turned way up and his eyes closed. He's not paying attention at all.

"Hi," I say.

"Hey." I can hear Cat breathing. "Jane, I don't know how to tell you this."

"Tell me what?"

"You say you got a letter from your mom? About going to rehab?"

"Yeah. Yesterday. Said she checked into some facility near Duluth."

"That—I don't think that can be right," Cat says. "Because I saw her just today. At the . . . at the liquor store."

"No," I say quickly, trying to piece the timing together in my head. "You must have seen her before she left." My mom sent the FedEx two days ago, saying she was leaving for rehab immediately. She called me yesterday when the package got re-routed, sounding lucid. Wouldn't that mean she'd called from the facility? In any case, she'd at least be in the rehab center by *today*. So Cat couldn't have seen her at the liquor store.

"My mom and I were at that Hallmark in Mills Plaza," Cat says. Her voice is so low, I can hardly hear her above the wind battering the van. "It's right next to a Petco? There's a First Round Liquors there too. And, Jane, I swear—we saw your mom come out of it."

"What time?" I whisper.

"I don't know. Around noon, I guess."

"There must be a mistake," is all I can think to say.

"Jane." Cat's voice loses some of its softness. "Just *think*. Think about what you're saying. I'm sorry to be the one to tell you this. But there is no way your mom is in rehab. She's not."

"But—she *has* to be." I grab the water bottle next to my seat and take a swig, suddenly parched.

"Why?" Cat asks.

"Because then she'll be better. And I can come home."

"Okay, but even if your mom went to rehab, which she didn't, it probably would be good for you to stay there anyway. You know? Just get some space. Let her figure out things on her own for a while."

Cat is saying the same thing Ethan had said. Which was the same thing Max had hinted at too. Was I really so wrong about all this?

"But—Jesus, Cat. I mean, if what you're saying is true, think about how in pain someone has to be to fake rehab. How screwed up. It's probably because I'm *down here* that she's doing all that. I can't just sit here while she goes all *Leaving Las Vegas* at the liquor store."

"Yes. Yes, you can. It's not up to you to fix her."

"But what if she dies? I mean, she could drink too much and pass out and choke on her own vomit."

"That's been a possibility all along. If you're really so worried now, call a neighbor. Have the cops come in and check on her. But don't go home."

I've never heard Cat sound so cold.

"She's faking rehab! It's a cry for help! She needs someone!"

"A trained professional, Jane. But not you."

I shake my head. "I don't know how you can be so dense about this. I just—I can't stand by and wait for my mom to *die*."

"If you come home now, you'll only make things worse."

"In *your* eyes."

"And in my eyes," Cat says, "if you come home, then we can't be friends."

"*Enough* with you and your rules," I cry. "Screw you and your note! You don't know how things are. It's not *your mom*!"

Cat hangs up with a click.

From the front seat, Victor turns around. "Everything okay? Were you just yelling?"

"I'm fine," I say, not looking at him. "Forget it."

For a second, Victor doesn't move. Then, slowly, he faces front again.

I'm so pissed at Cat, I dig my nails into my palms until they leave deep welts. Tears are pooling in my eyes, but I won't let them fall. I absolutely will not bawl. I just need to think. I need to figure out when I can get back to Minnesota. My mom needs me, and the Torbros hate me. There's never been a better time to exit stage left.

Outside the van, Stephen is motioning with his hands. "Check Polly, and let's head out!" he says. "The twister's gone, and looks like rain might move in after all. We need to get off this road!"

The back of the van opens up. Ethan and Mason slide Polly in, then slam the doors shut. Within seconds, we're tearing down the dirt road, trying to beat the rain. The whole team is chatting about the twister. Even Victor's asking questions.

I'm in the backseat, invisible once again. Which, for the first time all day, is fine with me. It means no one will notice when I get the hell out of here.

27

That night, we land at a motel in Shawnee, Oklahoma. When I look at a map in the lobby, I'm relieved to see the town isn't too far from Oklahoma City. I figure if I can get there, I can find transportation home. A bus, a train, a plane—something.

The minute I'm locked inside my musty room, I open my suitcase on the bed and unzip the inside pocket. I pull out the money I've saved from Ethan's paychecks, plus the little bit of cash I'd pooled together from babysitting jobs before I left. I count it twice, just to make sure I have the exact amount. It comes to $274.

Outside of getting robbed, I know I can get home on that with cash to spare. Easy.

A soft knock at the door has me shoving all the money underneath my clothes. When it's buried, I squint through the peephole and am surprised to see Hallie standing outside.

"Can I help you?" I ask, not opening the door.

"Jane, come on," she says. She pulls off her cowboy hat and

holds it in her hands like a gentleman caller or something. "We need to talk."

"About what?"

"Come on. Don't do this. Just open up."

Reluctantly, I turn the lock and crack the door. "What?"

"You're not going to invite me in?" she asks.

"Probably not."

"Fine," she says. "Then I just came by to tell you not to take what happened this morning too hard. Stephen's upset he's losing the other half of the Tornado Brothers. But he doesn't blame you for telling Max about Victor. No one does. At the end of the day, this is Victor's doing, not yours."

"Oh!" I say, smiling as if I'm finally getting a punch line that had eluded me all day. "Is that it?" I laugh. "Then, okay! Everything is totally fine!"

Hallie shifts her cowboy hat in her hands. "Are you upset because Max blabbed all this?"

My anger rises. "I'm *upset*, Sherlock, because everyone was a total asshat to me today. Including you. And guess what? I don't need it. I don't care about any of it. Not about the Torbros or storms or Polly or the Blisters or the stupid Weather Network. So whatever. Have fun with my brother and enjoy yourselves. I hope your lives turn out *great*. I hope you catch a zillion tornadoes. Best of luck to you. Just leave me out of it."

Hallie blinks. "Jeez. Hostile much?"

"You came to me, Hallie," I say, losing patience. "I didn't even want to have this conversation. But you're here. So I'm not just going to say, 'Oh, no problem, everyone can be a jerk to me for an entire day, but it's totally cool.' Because it's not cool at *all*."

"We were just upset," Hallie says. "The group's been chasing together a long time is all. Victor wasn't always this way, and it's been hard for us to admit that having him in the field wasn't just going to work itself out. So, excuse us if we had to blow off some steam for a while. But that doesn't mean you're not one of us. It doesn't mean anyone hates you."

"Huh," I say. "Could have fooled me."

Hallie purses her lips. "What's really going on here?" she asks after a moment. "You don't seem like yourself."

"That's probably because you don't know me."

Hallie sighs and puts her cowboy hat back on. "We're eating at the Golden Corral across the street tonight. We'd all like it if you'd join us."

"Thanks, but I think I'll be dining in," I say. I don't tell her I have a trip to plan. I don't tell her I hope I'm gone within twenty-four hours.

"Suit yourself," she says.

I slam the door.

While everyone is across the street eating, I duck into the motel's "business center," which in this case is more like a closet with a giant computer that looks older than I am. I wait for what feels like an hour as the thing boots up, its processor grinding.

The second I have an Internet connection, I start researching bus routes into Oklahoma City. There's one out at 4:14 P.M. tomorrow, arriving in Oklahoma City around six. The bus stop is a few miles away, but it's totally walkable. If I leave at three, I'll be there in plenty of time.

The trick, of course, will be evading the Torbros long enough to actually get *on* the bus. Plus, if they want to pack up early tomorrow and chase weather, there's no chance I'll be able to sneak away. If, on the other hand, they sit around and wait to see what the weather will do, I might have a shot.

Either way, I tell myself, if it doesn't work out tomorrow, it could work out the day after. Or the day after that. Even a town like Patchy Falls would have a bus. Or a taxi. And all those can take me somewhere with bigger modes of transportation—big enough to get back to Minnesota.

I just hope I can get back before anything drastic happens. On a whim, I pull out my cell and dial my mom. The phone rings and rings, then goes into voice mail. I scroll through my contacts and find our neighbor Henry. I click Talk.

He picks up on the third ring. "Yeah?"

"Henry. Hi, this is Jane McAllister? From next door?"

"Oh, yah. How you doin', Jane?"

"I'm fine, but I wonder if you might do me a favor and run next door to check on my mom. She . . ." My mind goes blank. The lies that used to come so easily aren't there anymore. I'm out of practice. I squeeze my eyes shut and concentrate. "She hasn't been feeling well," I continue, "and that flu medicine makes her so dizzy. I can't get in touch with her, and I'm worried she might have hit her head on the edge of the tub, you know?" I laugh, but it winds up sounding more like a grunt.

"Yah, sure," Henry says after a second. "I'll go check for you. You want me to go now?"

"If you don't mind. You can take the phone with you. I can just listen. If she answers the door, I'll know she's okay. But can you keep it a secret that I'm asking after her?" My mind races faster, thinking how awful my mom will feel if she knows *I* know she's not in rehab. "She doesn't like me checking up, so maybe you can just ask after the washing machine."

Henry mumbles something. Even though I can't quite make out what it is, I can probably guess. Something about this being overly complicated because, at the end of the day, I doubt I'm fooling him. After all, he's seen my mom wobble as she's pointed to the leaky faucet that needed repairing; she's slurred when explaining how the stove's pilot light doesn't work. He probably even saw her that day she was under the bushes. Henry probably knows exactly why I've phoned and what this is all about. But the pretenses are a part of it I just can't drop.

Maybe I'm only doing it to fool myself at this point, I think.

I hear him rap on the door. Then voices. I can only catch snippets. "Washer okay?" "Sweet of you." "Need just ask." Then the slam of the door, and Henry's back on the phone.

"You hear that? She's okay."

I breathe a little easier. "Thanks, Henry. I really appreciate it."

"You take care, Jane."

"I will."

We end the conversation, and that's that. I head back to my room, where my $274 sits tucked away, waiting for my big break. But before I get there, I get another text. This one from Max.

Where r u staying tonite? I'm ovr in Ada.

From staring at maps all day, I know that's southeast of here. A few days ago, I might have conjured up some kind of plan or scheme to go meet him. But now there's not a snowball's chance in a warm front. Not after what he did.

I don't reply, but another text comes through anyway.

Havnt heard from u all day. U ok?

Then another. **We stopped in a town 2day actually called Okay. LOL**

I can't bleve I said LOL.

LOLOLOL.

They won't stop.

Where r u?

Am I talking to the cosmos?

If ur mad at me, tell me, k?

I care abt u. I'm sorry if we left things weird. I'd like to c u agn. Somehow.

If u played the vortex game and it were me or the Pig & Spit, but only one cld survive a tornado, which wld u pik?

I kno their ribs are good, but I hope u pik me.

A laugh escapes my lips. How can he be so clueless about why I'm mad? How can he just pretend like nothing's wrong?

I force the smile off my face. I can't do this. I turn off my phone, once and for all.

But even after I hit the lights and curl into the cheap bed, my fingers itch to text him. Finally, I lie on my back and pin my hands underneath my head so I don't do anything stupid. After staring at the ceiling for what feels like hours, I finally fall asleep.

At breakfast the next morning, my first ray of hope that I might get back to Minnesota before next week comes in the form of bickering. Stephen and Ethan are standing next to a bucket of yogurts packed into ice, arguing that we should head north into Iowa. But Hallie and Mason disagree, saying it's best to stay put and watch potential activity to the west, which they say could put twisters into our backyard by sundown.

Bingo.

I grab a cup of coffee and am trying to really tune in to the details when I realize Victor's not in the mix.

"Hey," I say to Mason when their disagreement has simmered down, "is Victor around?"

"Naw," Mason says, shoving his hands into his pockets. "Left last night after dinner at the Golden Corral."

He's gone, and I didn't say good-bye. Because I was too pissed at the team to even have dinner with them.

I take a sip of java, telling myself it's a good thing he's gone. He's happier now. Even though that's true, it still doesn't make me feel any better.

My phone buzzes, and I stare at another text. **Hey u!** I figure at first it's Max again, but then I realize—it's my mom. At that moment everything goes quiet, and I'm not sure if it's because there's less noise in the room or because there's a roar in my ears that blocks out any other sound.

I simultaneously want to throw the phone across the room and hug it to my chest.

I punch the only reply I can think of: Hi mom! How r u?

I hit send and wait.

Gr8! The ppl at the rehab cntr r SO nice. They have ben helpfl & r letting me go early!!

I know it's a lie. But that's okay. I knew this was going to get messier before it would get simpler. That's awsm. I was thinking Id come hm & we cld hav the rest of the summer togethr.

Her response makes my stomach knot.

Naw, I am comng to c u. I have frequnt flyer miles. Am at the airprt, direct flight leavs in 20 min. Can u believe it?

It strikes me as almost funny that the biggest lie in that text is that she has frequent flyer miles. I've never known her to fly. Not once in all my seventeen years. So no way she's at the airport. Just like no way she got let out of rehab early.

The part that *isn't* funny is that she seems to be spiraling. The lies are getting worse. I need to get home fast before she does something seriously bad.

I ask her which airport she's flying into.

Oklahma City. Closest airprt to Ethan's house! R u nearby?

Actually yes, I type back. Dwn the road.

Gr8. When I get there, u will be first 2 kno.

Ok, I reply. Only after I hit Send do I realize the team's made a decision.

We're staying put for the time being.

By noon, I'm prowling around the motel, restless. Mason and Hallie made the right call—the radar shows strong potential for a tornado outbreak to the west—and any minute we might jump into the vans and chase. But we haven't done it yet. The possibility that we *could* is making little beads of sweat break out on my upper lip.

Should I wait until closer to three to make a break for it? Or leave now and risk them realizing I'm gone? I doubt they'll track me down—nobody cares that much—but still. What if they try?

God, Mom, I think. *Why does this have to be so complicated?*

Like she knows I'm thinking about her, my phone rings with her name in the caller ID. I hit Talk immediately.

"Mom?"

"Janey!" Her voice is so loud, I keep the phone a few inches from my ear. "I'm here! I made it!"

The motel hallway is suddenly sweltering. "What? How?"

"I flew! I *told* you! I bought a ticket, and I flew to see you!" I can tell from the way she's overarticulating her words that she's been drinking. She's trying too hard to sound sober. "This nice man from the airport brought me to my motel in a shuttle, and now I want to see you! I don't have a car, though. Can you drive here from wherever you are? Are you chasing close by, or will it take you a while to get here?"

Her voice is so loud. I don't remember her being this ear-splitting. "Mom, where's here?"

"I'm at the Super 8 on Shilling Road. In Oklahoma City!"

That's only twenty minutes away. If you're not taking the bus.

"I don't—I don't have a car," I say. "But then, it doesn't matter, right? You're not really there."

"What are you saying? Of *course* I'm here. I told you I was coming. When you pick me up, bring Ethan. Maybe he'll talk to me now that I've been to rehab."

My head is pounding. I'm having a hard time thinking.

"Mom, I just—I can't believe it. Is this really real? How did you get the money for the ticket?"

"Don't you worry about that, honey. I'm here, and that's all that matters. Now, get your brother and come see me. I'm at the Super 8 in room 211. On Shilling Road. Got it?"

I stall, confused. The details are so real. She's not usually this specific when she's lying. But how am I supposed to go see her? "I don't know, Mom—"

"I didn't fly all this way to hear *I don't know*. You can find a way. You're my smart girl."

I'm stunned into silence.

"I'll wait. When you get here, I'll be ready."

"Um. Okay?"

"Bye, honey. Love you, see you soon!"

My right eardrum is buzzing from all her yelling. I shove my cell phone in my pocket and make my way to the lobby, where the remaining Torbros are sprawled out, studying computers and radars. Cables and wires are everywhere in this makeshift base camp. The motel manager has even set up a pot of fresh coffee and a stack of Styrofoam cups for them.

Hallie's jiggling the van keys and staring at an atlas, like she's ready to drive away *now*.

"What's going on?" I ask.

"We've got action to the west," Ethan says. His gray-blue eyes are locked on the computer screen, his angular face focused. "We're watching it. If it keeps building, we're going to hit the road soon."

I glance out the window. It's not yet one o'clock, and the sun is bright. It looks like it's time to barbecue—not chase. But I know how quickly weather can change.

"Ethan," I say, "I need to talk to you." Hallie glances up at my tone.

"Now?" Ethan asks.

"It's important."

He leaves the computer, and we step over to a coffee table scarred with the pale rings of a hundred sweating drinks. "What's going on?" he asks.

"Mom called me."

"And?"

"She's here. In Oklahoma City. She wants to see us."

Ethan's eyes darken and narrow. "She's what?"

"She's here. At a Super 8. She just called me and wants us to come over."

Ethan throws his head back and laughs. The rest of the Torbros stop what they're doing to stare.

"This isn't funny," I say.

"The hell it's not," Ethan replies, running a hand through his hair. "Come on. Mom is here? Out of 'rehab' already?" He makes air quotes around the word *rehab*. "And she wants us to drop whatever we're doing to come see her? That's freaking hilarious."

"Well, help me figure it out," I snap. "We can go after the chase, I suppose. I mean, it'll probably be late, but I guess we could go after the storm loses steam."

Ethan laughs again, only this time it's clear he's less amused. "You're actually thinking about going to see her?"

"Of *course*," I reply. "If she lied about rehab, she did it for a reason. She could really be in trouble. We need to *check* on her."

Ethan's expression hardens. "We are not going to go see her. Under zero circumstances will we be driving anywhere near that Super 8. Do you understand?"

"What? Why?"

"Because, Jane, this is what she does. Don't you see? This is what I'm talking about. Mom creates messes and then brings you in to clean them up."

"Look, I know I have a role in all this. Fine. But we can't just leave her there in a Super 8. We don't even know how she's getting *home*."

Ethan throws up his hands. "And that's your problem?"

"Well, *yes*. I mean, at least a little bit."

"Why?" Ethan demands. "Did you invite her?"

"Not exactly."

"Did she arrange this with you?"

"No."

"Did you work out the details of her stay in advance?"

"No. Of course not."

"Then what obligation do you have to turn everything upside down and go to her? Don't you see? This is the same shit. *The same.* Every time."

"But we—we *have* to." My voice is getting tighter. Ethan's face softens a little.

"Jane, come on. Listen to me. This is the part where you need to break out of the cycle she's put you in. You have to stop focusing on helping her with her problems, so you can focus on *you.* Like what we talked about."

Except that was hypothetical. And this feels all too real.

"Don't go see Mom," Ethan says. "Let her be alone in that motel room. Okay?"

Like you left us alone in Minnesota, I think. I know I need to, but I can't let that *one fact* go—not even after Ethan's apologized, after he's invited me to live with him in Oklahoma. Because he's still got his checklist out, ticking off what we all need to do in order to fit into his perfect life. No way is a check ever going to go next to my name. My fuckup with Max yesterday certainly made that much obvious.

He's abandoning me again, I can hear my mom saying. *The same way he'll eventually abandon you.*

"Okay," I say, pretending I've made up my mind, that Ethan's gotten through to me. "I won't go."

"Good," Ethan says, clapping me on the back. "Now let's go get this storm."

He walks back to the Torbros, and I follow behind him, but

move toward the left, closer to Hallie and the free coffee. Her eyes flicker across my face. I know she's wondering what the heck is up. I also know that what I'm about to do is going to totally and completely suck for her.

Filling two cups to the brim with hot coffee, I walk toward the group with a plastic smile plastered to my face. "Anyone want coffee?" I ask, then lose my footing like I've tripped over a cable. "Oh!" I cry as hot coffee goes everywhere—but mostly all over Hallie.

"Ooooww!" she cries, bolting up from her seat. Her atlas slides off her lap and onto the floor. She drops the van keys and shakes off the burning liquid. "What are you doing?"

"Oh, my God, I'm so sorry," I say, bending down like I'm trying to get at the discarded cups. I scramble on the floor until I locate the van keys. I grab them, along with the atlas, and stand. "I'm such a total klutz," I say. "I'm really sorry."

Hallie's cheeks are pink. She's gorgeous, even when she's furious. "You want to borrow some clean clothes?" I ask. She just shakes her head, then heads off to her room. The other Torbros are watching me. "I'm really sorry," I say. I glance down and notice I'm covered with coffee as well. "Erm, I should probably go change." The group is silent as I walk away.

The minute I'm out of sight, I bolt for the nearest exit and hop into the Torbros van in the parking lot. I throw the atlas on the seat next to me, opened to a street-by-street grid of Oklahoma City. I start the engine and pray none of the Torbros are watching as I pull away.

28

I am in trouble. I am in the hugest, majorest trouble ever. This is all I can think as I speed down the interstate toward my mom.

"Oh, God," I groan. What am I *doing*?

I glance at my cell phone. It's quiet, which is a good thing. I figure it'll start blowing up the minute the Torbros decide to chase and find out they have no van.

I peer through the windshield and can't help but notice the clouds building. There really is going to be one heck of a storm soon. I just hope it's not *too* good, otherwise it'll be more salt in the Torbros' missing-van wound.

If my mom and this van were sucked up into a twister and only one could survive, I think suddenly, *which would it be?*

I must be losing it if I'm playing the vortex game now, I realize. But I think about the answer anyway.

This one's easy. I'd pick my mom.

The questions don't stop there. *If my mom or the president of the United States were sucked up into the twister, which would you pick?*

I shake my head. Why are my thoughts swirling like this? "That's an insane question," I say out loud. Now I'm really losing it, talking to myself. "You can't choose between your family and the leader of the free world." There's no response in the van. Did I expect there to be? "But I'd still pick my mom."

If you or your mom were sucked into a twister, and only one of you could survive, which would you pick?

The question sticks in my brain before I can take it back. My mom or me?

Both of you are in the twister. Who gets to live?

"That's a trick question!" I yell. You can't choose between yourself and family.

Can you?

Something like a sob is working its way up my throat. My lungs don't feel like they're working right. I'm going to go see my mom. So why am I blinking back tears?

I force myself to focus. The exit to my mom's motel is coming up. This is it. I'll be able to see her. The minute I lay eyes on her I'll know I've done the right thing.

Both of you are in the twister. Who gets to live?

I take my right palm and swipe it quickly over both my eyes. "Get a grip, Jane McAllister." I can see the Super 8 sign in the distance. I head through a few lights, then turn into the parking lot.

The minute I hop out onto the blacktop, the charge in the air sets my hairs on end. A storm is definitely rolling in. To the west, white clouds billow. The supercell is enormous. If it keeps building like this, it'll be one of the biggest storms we've seen all season.

I step inside the Super 8, vaguely aware it has the same smell as every other motel we've stayed at. It's a mixture of worn carpet, coffee, and stale air.

For a moment, I pause, half expecting someone to point at me and yell, "Stop that girl! She stole a van!" But nothing happens. The hallways are quiet as I pass by the front desk toward the elevators.

Trying to keep my hand from shaking, I punch floor two. As the elevator lifts, I tell myself there's a solid chance Mom's not actually here. That I'll pound on her door and nothing will happen. That I'll call her cell, but she won't answer. Later tonight, she'll text me and say she can't believe I fell for it.

The elevator doors open, and I step out, wondering if this is all a joke, will I be disappointed . . . or relieved?

I stand in front of room 211.

Both of you are in the twister. Who gets to live?

I raise my hand and knock.

My mom flings open the door with so much force, she actually staggers backward. She might also stagger because she's drunk.

"Jayyyneeeeey!" she squeals. Her arms cinch around me, and I feel her bones through her cheap tracksuit. After a year-long hug, she finally holds me out at arm's length and beams. "Aren't you a *sight*," she says. "Look at you."

"Look at *you*," I reply, taking in her hollowed cheeks, her dry hair, the deep circles under her eyes. I was right to come. She's in a bad way. "Can I come in?"

"Oh, like you have to ask? This is your room now too. I figure we'll stay together for a while, right?"

I don't answer as I enter. Clothes are strewn on the bed, on the desk chair, on the floor. The bathroom light is on, and the water is running. There's an empty wine bottle on the nightstand. "How long have you been here?" I ask.

"About an hour now," she answers.

I pick up a few of the clothes on the floor and lay them on the bed. Only an hour, and already she's made it look like she's been living here for days. I wonder what shape our apartment is in back in Minnesota.

My mom leans against the dresser, loses her balance, then finds it again. "So I take it Ethan couldn't be bothered to come see me," she says. She grabs a nearby cup and drains the last few drops out of the bottom.

"He's busy with a chase."

"It's okay," my mom says in a tone that indicates it's not. "I know what he thinks about me. I know he can't be bothered with his *family*."

I open the blinds and let in the fading afternoon light. "It's not like that," I say.

"What, so you've spent a few weeks with him, and now

you hate me too?" She gives me a pointed look, then walks unsteadily to her suitcase, where she pulls out another bottle of wine. She twists off the top, then goes back to her empty cup on the dresser and fills it.

"No one hates you," I say, watching her drink. "We hate your problem. For which I thought you were going to rehab. You wrote me a letter. Remember?"

My mom sets down the plastic cup. "I did go to rehab. I was there for a little while and realized I don't need a clinic to make me better. I'm actually getting better on my own."

My heart slams inside my chest. "Mom, why are you lying? We both know you didn't go to rehab. So why'd you make it up? Did something happen?"

My mom lifts her chin. "Not all of it was a lie. I did get five-hundred dollars from work, you know."

"For what?"

"For being an exemplary employee. For being someone the other girls look up to."

"Mom, *tell me*. What was the money for?"

Mom swirls the liquid in her cup. We watch it roll around and around, a tiny tempest.

"Mom?"

"Severance," she says finally, like it's a fancy term she's letting roll over her tongue at a garden party.

I suddenly need to sit. I make it to the edge of the bed before my legs collapse. "You were fired?"

"Not fired. They called it a reduction in force."

"You don't have—a job?"

"Not yet." She straightens her sweatshirt, picks some imaginary lint off her fuzzy track pants. "But I'm looking. I think I might want to switch careers. Maybe become a pilot."

"Mom. Stop. You can't be a pilot."

"Says who?"

"Says me!" I cry, standing up.

My mom's head jerks back a little. I almost never yell at her. "Janey," she says, "I'm not trying to be difficult. I don't want to upset you."

"You should have thought about that before you lost your job!" I reply. "What are we supposed to do now? How are we going to pay the rent?"

My mom swallows more wine. "I can get another one. Easy. I'll work at the grocery store. I know Diana up at the SaveMore. She can get me something. We'll move to a smaller apartment. We'll make it work. We always do."

"But you'll keep drinking," I say. "Or worse. Other drugs maybe? Right?"

Her head jerks, like something's landed on her but she can't be bothered to raise a hand and swat it away. She takes a wobbly step toward me. Then another. Right then I think how strange it is that she's wobbling, loose like a noodle, when the rest of her is so brittle. Her hair, her nails. Even her skin looks like it might crack away from her bones in flat, hard pieces.

"Honey, I'm getting better. Can't you see that? And now that you're back, I'll be *fine*. We're a team, right? You and me."

"This is what you look like when you're getting better?" I ask.

"Well, you wouldn't know how much worse it's been lately," Mom says, setting down her drink. "You haven't been around."

"I left because of what you did to Cat. To *me*. You could have killed us."

Mom scowls. "That bullshit? I've been in worse accidents than that."

"Well, I haven't. And neither has Cat."

"So that gives you the right to bolt? Every time something bad happens you get to take off?"

I look at the door. Right then, I want to leave so badly, the muscles in my legs ache. They're screaming at me to just sprint away. Run and run and run and never look back.

But this is what I wanted, I tell myself. I knocked on that door and signed up to help my mom, who clearly needs me now more than ever. Except Ethan's words are worming their way through my brain, and the gnawing feeling in my marrow tells me he's right: Mom's never going to get help if I don't change. If I don't stop waiting on her, I'm going to empty myself, bit by bit, until I'm nothing but a dried-out husk. And it's never going to change. Unless I *make* it change.

"How did you plan on getting home, Mom?" I ask.

My mom closes her eyes. "Let me think. Let me seeeeee . . ." She opens her eyes. "I guess I was thinking we could stay here for awhile, take in the sights, then ride the Amtrak back or something. A mommy-daughter road trip!"

Behind my mom, outside the window, I can see the supercell looming. As if on cue, my cell phone buzzes.

When I hit Talk, Ethan's voice erupts in my ear. "Jane, goddamn it, what the hell are you doing?"

I stare at my mom, my eyes filling up with tears. "I stole your van."

"I can goddamn well see that! Are you out of your mind? You're not authorized to drive it. What's more, we need it! And, for crying out loud, you stole it to be with Mom, which is—"

My mom grabs the phone out of my hands. "Ethan, this is your mother. You stop yelling at Janey right now. I can hear you from across the room."

I hear Ethan hollering at her now, but I can't make out what he's saying. I can only imagine.

"Whatever she did," my mom retorts, "it's because she *loves* me, which is more than I can say for you . . . Well, she's here in this motel room, and you're not . . . All you care about is . . . I'm tired of your godda—" My mom stops talking and hands the phone to me. "He hung up."

"What'd he say?"

"Same crap about how I'm a horrible mother. How I'm ruining you. How he needs his stupid van back."

I look out the window. The storm is gorgeous—the bottom of the sharp-edged clouds is golden in the setting sunlight, billowing to pink, then white as they rise up, up, up. In that moment, *everything* is in clear relief.

I reach into my back pocket and pull out my wallet. I grab all the money I have—$274—and shove it at my mom. "Here."

She glances at it with bleary eyes. "Keep that," she says, waving me away clumsily. "We're going to need it for the road. I figure we can probably get to the train station before they find us."

I stare at her, grief filling my every pore. "No, Mom," I whisper. "I'm not going to drive us to the train station. I'm not going to take you anywhere. You're going to have to get home on your own."

She puts a hand on her bony hip. Her thin fingers drum out a beat, her nails flashing bright red. "Don't be stupid," she says. "We're leaving together. I *can't* leave without you. I can't leave without my Janey."

I shake my head, the tears pouring down my face. "I can't do it," I say. "I can't go home with you. I can't—I can't *take care* of you."

My mom grunts. "Of course you can. You always have. We take care of each other. It's you and me, baby."

Words feel sticky in my mouth, like they don't want to come out. "No, Mom. I'm done."

"So, what? You're going to stay here with Ethan? Like he's so much better than me?"

"No," I say. "Maybe. I don't know."

Both of you are in the twister. Who gets to live?

My body is so heavy, I want to lie down. My grief is lead. My thoughts are iron. If I'm not careful, I'm going to fall out of the tornado and crash to the ground.

And then I wonder if that's such a bad thing. How else do you get out of the tornado in the vortex game? How else do you survive except by falling?

"Tell me the truth," I say. "Tell me what you're into besides alcohol. Which drug?"

Mom blinks so much, her eyelids remind me of window shades going up and down, again and again. "Nothing. I'm not doing anything else. Don't be stupid."

I let one second pass. Then another. My heart slows. I can feel each beat, feel every breath filling my lungs. She is lying. I know it like I know I am alive, standing in this room, on this brown carpet.

This is how it has to be, I realize. The horrible heaviness of the truth is on me, and I can't fight it anymore. I have to weld myself to it. Either I do that and the tornado drops me, or I die spinning in its insanity.

It's time to make myself so substantial, the tornado can no longer hold me. It's time to fall back to Earth.

I wipe the tears off my cheeks and take a breath. "I don't know how this is going to work," I say. "I don't know how to not be in the twister without you. But I have to try."

"What the hell are you talking about?" Mom asks. She takes a long swallow of her drink, clutching her glass like she might get blown away if she lets go of it. "English, please."

"It's the vortex game. You and me. We're in a twister. And only one of us gets to survive. Who is it?"

My mom glances at the cash, still in my hand. Her eyes narrow as her brain tries to wrap itself around what I'm saying. "You telling me you're headed to a chase right now? With all that money?"

"No. I'm trying to explain how the vortex game works."

She takes the cash from me. "You know who survives? The one who understands exactly what to do when the chips are down. That would be *me*. I'm *cut out* for this survival stuff, Janey. But you? The world is going to eat you alive. Without me, you think you can survive but you can't. Hear me? You *can't*."

She might be right. I might die, tumbling out of the twister like this. But there's no life left for me if I stay in the swirling chaos either.

I move toward the door. I'm so weighted, it's hard to put one step in front of the other. I swear there are stones in my blood. I will my hair to become steel shavings, my bones to become metal rods. I am the heaviest human being who ever lived, and the tornado can't hold me.

"You're stuck with me," Mom says. "You can't leave me."

"I can," I say, even though my tongue is copper. "I have to go."

Although I'm slow, Mom doesn't try to stop me. She just stands there with her drink in one hand, the cash in the other.

"So that's it?" she asks. "Because don't think for one hot second you can walk out that door, then come back and live with me."

I turn the door handle. My mom throws her plastic cup at me. Wine splatters on the wall, on my clothes. It reminds me of the blood on Cat's white floor after the accident. I can feel the glass, all over again—only this time in my heart, not my face, slicing my arteries and ventricles into pieces. "You can't go!"

For a second, I think she's right. I've made myself too heavy. I am going to be stuck here, forever, trapped in this motel room with Mom. But then the door is open, and it's a little easier to move again. I'm weighted, but I'm not broken.

"Bye, Mom," I whisper.

With my iron hand, I close the door to 211 behind me, and exit the Super 8.

29

The farther away I get from the Super 8, the lighter I become. But my heart is still shredded, and my veins feel like they're still pumping shavings.

I drive along the highway, glancing at the atlas and trying to remember how to get back to Shawnee. I'm behind the storm, tailing it, and I know that if the Torbros were here, they'd be screaming with excitement at the nearby wall cloud that's getting lower and lower.

But they're not here. Thanks to me.

Tears course down my cheeks, and I wipe them away so I can still see the road. What a disaster.

I wonder if Ethan will ever forgive me.

More than that, I wonder if Ethan will still want me to come live with him.

That idea that the answer might be no clutches at my ragged heart.

I look to the right and spot a long line of weather tourist vans parked hood to bumper, watching the nearby wall cloud blacken and churn. There's no funnel cloud yet, but I'm betting there will be soon.

An idea sparks just as the exit ramp appears. I signal and pull off the highway, my heart racing.

I might have screwed up the Torbros' chase, but I can still help them. Polly is still in the back, and if I'm careful, I bet I can put her right in the middle of the storm and get amazing data. She'll get all kinds of new information before the Blisters can build their own prototype and scoop us. If I come back with a hard drive full of new numbers, Ethan can't stay mad. We'll make a clean start toward . . . wherever it is we go from here.

I race past the tourist vans, who honk at me. They might be afraid to get too close, but I'm not. I'm getting close enough to make this right. As if on cue, a funnel cloud starts spinning. And at the same time, my phone buzzes. I yank it out of my pocket and put it on speaker so I can keep both hands on the wheel.

"Jane!" It's my brother again. "Stop the fucking van right now. I can't believe you and Mom left the Super 8."

"Not Mom," I say. "Just me."

"What the hell? You're alone?"

I was alone, all right—big time. "Yes."

Ethan's silent for a second. "Jane, where are you *going*?"

"Up to the storm. Looks like there's a funnel about a mile

ahead." Cars going the other way down the road are flashing their lights at me, but I keep driving.

"Okay," Ethan says, and I can hear him trying to control his tone. "I need you to pull the van over right now. We're behind you, and we can see you on the GPS, but you need to stop driving. *Now.* Do you understand?"

"I will. I'll stop, Ethan, I swear. But right now, I have to get Polly out there so she can collect all that data you need. So I can make all this up to you."

"Polly? What the hell are you talking about? Jane, don't touch Polly. Just stop the van. Look, I'm not mad. Okay? If I promise you I'm not mad, will you stop?"

I shake my head. "No. I have to do this."

"Jesus, Jane. What the hell happened with Mom? Did you snap or something?"

"No, of course not." There's a roar in my ears, and I realize it's the storm. I'm awfully close.

There's a fumbling sound, then a pause. I hear a breath. "Jane, this is Max."

I lift my foot off the accelerator just a touch. "Max," I say. I can't slog through the logic of any of this. "Why are you on Ethan's phone?"

"The Torbros called us when their van went missing. And now we're chasing you."

"Oh." I slow way down, in part to concentrate on Max, and in part because there's a road to my right that looks like it might take me closer to the funnel.

"Why are you talking to me?" I ask.

"Because I'm trying to help you," Max replies. "You need some major, supercell-sized help right now."

My blood heats up. "Why are you trying to save the day when you were the one who told Alex what I said about Victor?"

"Except I didn't. The Weather Network was recording us by the pool without us knowing. I never said jack. They just showed their dailies to Alex."

The van inches along. "The Weather Network?" I ask. "They were filming us?"

"Yeah. I think we gave them quite a show. If you come home, we can watch the footage together. Laugh about it until we decide to rip Alex Atkins's head off."

It strikes me then that he might be lying. He might be telling me all this just to get me to stop the van.

I stare down the road to my right. "I can see it now," I say to Max. "The twister, I mean." My hands are shaking so much, I can hardly grip the steering wheel. "It looks different this close. Not really as defined. Less like a funnel and more like if someone stuck gauze in a blender."

Max lowers his voice. "God, Jane. You're really close. Please stop, okay? Stop the van."

I'm trying to follow along. He's right. I need to stop the van to get Polly out into the field so she can take readings. "Okay," I say. "I have to hang up now, but I'll call you back."

Max's words tumble out, fast and loud. "Wait! Jane. Don't

hang up! Do *not* do this. You are going to get seriously hurt. Look, we're only a couple minutes behind you. Stay in the van, and we'll be right there."

I want to point out that I can't. I've come this far—I might as well finish the job. But I don't get the chance. Our signal is gone. I need to get Polly into the field ASAP, so I turn down the road to my right, and panic only a little when I realize it's dirt. And it's started to rain. I force myself to press down on the accelerator.

I can see the filmy chaos of the tornado's base up ahead. I put the van in park, and open the door, except I can't open it because the wind is too ferocious. I kick at it with my feet and, after a few seconds of grunting, the door catches the wind and almost flies off its hinges. It groans and creaks. The minute I step out of the van, the wind pushes me into the mud.

I crawl toward the back of the van, desperate to unload Polly. I feel the wind tearing up the sleeves of my shirt, feel flecks of dirt stinging my face, the wind turning them into tiny projectiles. I clutch at the van's rear tire. But at the same time, I turn my head and stare at the screaming haze. Just a few yards in the opposite direction, and I'd be there. I'd be right there at the tornado's edge, and I could let go. I'm not heavy anymore. I'm just Jane. I'm all alone, and I'm not playing the vortex game.

Maybe it's time to know what it feels like to get sucked into the sky. I imagine the spinning, the flailing, the total lack of control. It would be such a relief, I think, after having to make myself so very weighted.

In the wind, I hear a cry. "Don't move!"

I raise my head, and there's Ethan. His eyes are huge and afraid, and he's crawling toward me. "Just stay there!" he yells. "I'm coming for you!"

A few yards behind Ethan, Max is struggling in the ferocious air. Behind Max is Hallie. I think I can make out Mason and Stephen. The *entire team* is out in the storm, trying to save me.

And then it hits me. The reckless, insane enormity of what I'm doing out here comes crashing down on me so hard, I lose my breath. I might die. *Ethan* might die. The entire Torbros team might die, *plus Max*. And not by accident, like what happened with Victor steering them too close to a funnel. But on purpose because I barreled headlong into the wind like the most selfish, reckless person who ever lived.

I'm a shaking mess when Ethan finally reaches me. "Listen to me!" he yells. "We have to move! Do you understand?" I nod, figuring we're going to run away from the van, but instead he pushes me toward it. He all but shoves me into the open door that looks like it might come sailing off its hinges at any second. I climb into the van just as glass from the windshield and side doors shatters and hits me. I scream and cover my face. Glass is everywhere. Just like with Cat. Just like with Victor. If anything flies through the window now, I'll be dead.

Waving frantically at everyone else to get back into the Blisters' Escalade, Ethan throws himself inside our van behind me. He doesn't even try to shut the door. A log the length of a canoe goes sailing past the hood. A few more feet, and it would have hit the van, probably killing us. "Go!" I holler. "Drive!" Ethan starts the engine and throws the van in reverse. He looks at me, and his mouth is moving, but I don't hear the sound above the wind. Which is fine with me. As long as I hear the roar, I'm alive. When everything goes quiet, then we're really going to be in trouble.

When there's only silence, I'll be dead.

30

The tornado's shrieking all around us as we fishtail down the dirt road in reverse. We slide and slip, the sloppy mess eating away at our traction. Ethan's hands are locked on the steering wheel.

My insides liquefy as metal screeches above us. It's the scream of wounded animals. The next thing I know, one of the antennae from the van's roof is tumbling past us, bent to hell. A sharp wind gust sends dirt and leaves flying into the van, and I swat at them just so I can see. "We're almost there!" Ethan shouts.

We hit the paved road with a bump that sends me flying out of my seat. I grab on to Ethan as he whips the van around, then throws it into drive. The engine roars as we take off ahead of the twister. I watch through the cracked rear windshield as the twister grows smaller and smaller. I don't turn around until it's disappeared entirely.

Two miles later, we pull the van over behind the Blisters'

black Escalade, which looks more gray than anything now, thanks to the thick coating of mud it's wearing. The tornado has petered out, and the sky is opening up. Golden rays from the evening sun are pouring through the patchy clouds.

Ethan turns to me. He has mud and leaves and sticks in his hair. His clothes are ripped in places. His face is six shades darker thanks to all the dirt. And his door is *still open*.

I expect him to open his mouth and start yelling at me, lecturing me about the horrible, dangerous, reckless, *insane* thing I just did. But instead, he just bursts into tears.

My brother. Is *crying*.

I've barely ever seen him sad, much less teary.

Within seconds, I'm sobbing too. Ethan reaches out and gathers me into his arms. "I'm so sorry," he cries into my shoulder. "I'm so sorry for all of this. I should have been there for you, and I wasn't. I let you down. And I was such a jerk, not going with you to see Mom." Ethan pulls away, and there are white tear stains tracked through the dirt on his face. "Jane, I'm so sorry I made you feel like the only option you had was to face down a tornado. That I made you think that's all there *was*."

I shake my head. Why is Ethan apologizing? "No, no. I'm the one who screwed everything up. I just—I stopped thinking. The only thing that made sense was getting Polly close to the twister. But then you showed up. I would have *died*, and I don't even think I realized I was in such a horrible place. You . . . you saved my life."

Ethan wipes his face with his T-shirt sleeve, then shakes his head. "I'm sorry if I've been hard on you. I just wanted you to have a better life. From the minute I left, it tore me up me to know you were stuck back in that piece-of-shit apartment with Mom. I've always wanted you down here, and I still do."

Ethan's eyes are bloodshot and pained.

"Even after what I just did? You still want me?"

Ethan nods and gives me another hug. "It just shows me how much you need me. And how much I need you. Our family's pretty fucked up, Jane. I gotta say. But I think, maybe if you and I stick by each other and help each other out, we'll be okay."

I reach into the glove box for some napkins to blow my nose. I hand the remainder to Ethan so he can do the same.

"We just hired Max, by the way," Ethan says after a minute.

"What?"

"He took that Twister Blisters' Escalade without authorization. Just like you took *our* van without authorization. He heard us over the CB radioing in our situation, and then he basically heard Alex Atkins tell us to go fuck ourselves. Max didn't like that option. So he did what you did. He stole the keys, got the SUV, and came to get us."

I start at the realization that Max just threw away his Twister Blisters internship to save me. "He says we were taped," I say. "That he never told Alex about Victor. The Weather Network crew did."

Ethan nods. "Yeah. Max says it took him a while to figure out what Alex had said to you, that he played it like Max was in on the whole thing. But he wasn't."

"You believe him?" I ask.

"I'm not sure it matters what I believe," Ethan says. "I think it matters what *you* believe."

"I don't know." This all seems like a lot after we've just survived a tornado. And besides, even if I did decide that Max was telling the truth, there's still the sticky matter of what happens with us after the season wraps.

"Jane," Ethan says, like he knows what I'm thinking, "I'm no expert here. But I think any guy who risks his life to help save you might be worth taking a chance on. You don't have to figure it all out now. You don't have to know how the story ends. But you might have to give it a chance to unfold."

I nod, hoping I haven't screwed everything up beyond repair. "Unless Max thinks I'm completely out of my mind."

"Well, what you did just now sure *was* five shades of batshit crazy," Ethan says. "You need therapy, Jane. Like, for real. It will do you a lot of good to talk to someone."

I look at the floor mats until Ethan grabs my chin and directs my gaze at him. "I think I could use some myself, so I'll make you a deal. How about we go together for the first few sessions?"

Somehow, facing counseling with Ethan makes it seem less scary. Maybe I wasn't ready to tackle all the demons myself, but between the two of us, we could slay a few together.

"Okay," I say. "I can deal with that."

Ethan smiles. "For what it's worth, I think psychiatrists know that everyone who hunts storms is a little crazy. Maybe all the Torbros should go, huh? Find out what we're all chasing in our subconscious."

Tears spill out of my eyes all over again. "God. The team. Do they hate me?"

Ethan grabs my hand. "Jane. They just braved what I'm guessing was an EF-3 to save you. They're family. Same as me. That's how it is with chasers. We go into the storms with each other. *For* each other. Yeah, we fight. Yeah, we piss each other off too. But that's what happens with families. The difference between the Torbros and what you're used to is that the responsibility for fixing a situation doesn't fall entirely to you. People who really have your back might let things get messy for a while, but not for too long. People who really care about you will help mend fences. They'll get in the dirt with you. The thing is, you gotta let 'em help when they show up."

I nod, thinking about slamming the door in Hallie's face the other night at the hotel. *Next time,* I think, *I'll let her in.*

At the sound of approaching voices, Ethan jumps out his still-open van door, and I do the same. The Torbros—plus Max—are running toward us. The whole lot of us are muddy, cut, ripped, and bruised, but it doesn't matter. The next thing I know, we're clasped together, a sea of bodies and arms, and I'm smack in the middle of it.

It's an EF-5-sized group hug, and nothing in the whole world has felt as good as this.

31

I pull my new tank top on and smooth out the lines on my jeans. I turn back and forth in front of the mirror, my ponytail swooshing with each move. On a whim, I clip an oversized flower barrette from the seventies into my hair. "You can do this," I say out loud—hoping the sound of my own voice will neutralize any doubt that I'm ready for my first day at a brand-new school.

My cell phone rings, and I hit Talk. "Hey, you," I say to Cat.

"Hey," she says. "Are you nervous?"

My eyes dart around my bedroom, taking in the sparse furniture, the posters tacked up at odd angles, the futon that has to be my bed until Ethan and I can afford a real one for me. Despite how makeshift it all looks, something about it feels exactly right.

"I'm pretty freaked," I admit. "Plus, did you know Oklahoma is still, like, blazing hot this time of year? I'm used to it being at least a little cool when school starts in the fall."

Cat laughs. "Well, let's hope it stays that way, and then I can bring my bikini when I come visit in a few weeks."

"I'll let you know if I spot some choice boys who might want to see you in it," I say.

"The choicest boy is Max, and we all know he's taken," Cat says.

"Yeah, he is. But he's also in school in upstate New York. Guess you and I will have to make do with each other."

"I think I can handle that. In the meantime, kick ass today. I miss you."

"Miss you too," I say, thinking how weird it will be for Cat and me to be going to classes a thousand miles apart today. Then again, part of me is just glad we're still talking. After the twister, I'd called her and apologized, and told her she was right—about everything. But that I was ready to change things. Between the move to Oklahoma, the fact that Ethan and I were going to Dr. Paul, our new counselor, and that I'd started attending Al-Anon meetings, everything on Cat's list was officially checked off.

Not that it was ever about the specific tasks per se. It was more about me figuring out that helping someone doesn't always come wrapped in the package you think it does.

The vortex game wasn't entirely correct, after all. When you're in the twister with someone you love, you don't have to decide who gets to live and who gets to die.

You can get out of the tornado altogether.

"IM me later?" Cat says.

"For sure."

We hang up just as Ethan calls to me from the bottom of the stairs. "Jane! Let's go! I need to drop you off, then get to the lab."

I barrel down the stairs, and Ethan smiles. "Ready for your first day of school?"

"You sound like I'm six years old."

"I *feel* like you're six years old. Is that weird?"

"Yes," I say, "especially because I'm making dinner tonight."

"You know it's not just me, right?"

"Dur," I say. "I am totally aware Hallie's coming over. That's why I'm cooking."

"My only request is, don't make the meal too heavy. We thought we might go over some of Victor's latest field designs, and we can't do that if a bellyful of pasta is making us sleepy."

I laugh. "I know Victor's engineering is amazing, but can't you guys ever just have a regular date? Seriously. Like, pop in a movie, light some candles, and send me upstairs to do my homework? Is that too much to ask?"

Ethan bows. "For she who secured us victory in the bet, I concede."

"No, we still lost," I clarify. "But we did catch a break." As it turned out, the story of how I got us as close to the twister as I did—close enough to smell its farts, as Mason likes to joke—traveled through the chasing community faster than lightning. At first I was mortified—I was *that* girl, the crazy one who lost her marbles and drove straight into a funnel. But when the Weather Network heard about it, especially the part about the entire team coming to my rescue, they decided that, lost bet or no, maybe we were the kind of chasers they ought to be following a bit more closely. Besides, the producers said the footage of Victor running away from Danny, then working to help the town, of Ethan fixing the Culvers' barn shirtless and line dancing with Hallie, and of all of us cleaning up Patchy Falls side by side with the Blisters, was some of the best stuff they got all season. Next year, they agreed they'd track us solo on at least a few chases. We might not have black Escalades yet, but it's a start.

"I wish the Network would let us know when they want to start rolling tape in the spring," Ethan says. "You'd think they'd have already picked a date. Wouldn't you?"

"It might be a game-time decision, depending on how warm or cold the spring is," I offer. "Besides, if you could, you'd be out there in February chasing."

Ethan grins. "Twisters in the winter? It could happen."

"And you'd be the first one out there to catch them. Except, in the meantime, we have other things to worry about. Like getting me to school on time. And the daily picture."

"Right," he says. "You ready for that now?"

"Ready," I reply, and he holds his phone out at arm's length. I lean my head into Ethan's, and we both smile. He snaps the picture, punches a few buttons, then hits Send. The picture goes to my mom's phone with the same words every time: *We love you. Get better.*

We take the same picture every day.

Every day, I tell her that when she's better, I'll come back.

Every day, I hope she'll tell me she's trying. So far, that

243

hasn't happened yet, but I haven't lost hope. In fact, I hold tight to hope, especially on the days when I have to remind myself it's not up to me to save my mom. There are moments I have to fight the desire to fly back to Minnesota and make sure she's working her new gig at the grocery store and paying her bills and eating. But I bat it back because I know now: there's a fine line between saving someone and helping them destroy themselves.

Ethan pulls up to the school and turns down the radio. "You have your class schedule?" he asks.

"I'm a senior. I'll be fine. This isn't my first time at the rodeo."

"Look at you," Ethan says, "talking like you're from Oklahoma already."

"Speaking of, if I'm really going to fit in down here, then you need to teach me to line dance."

Ethan grins. "We'll talk," he says. "Now, get going."

I hop out of his truck, wave, and head toward the dust-colored two-story high school like it's nothing. I've faced down an EF-3. How bad can a new school be?

Just before I get to the double doors, my cell phone rings.

"Picture a twister out on the plains," Max says, like he does every day, "and say you know it's going to suck up two things. Your brand-new high school or the e-mail you have waiting from me when you open your in-box. Which do you pick?"

"You wrote me an e-mail?"

"You say that like I don't write you e-mails every day."

I watch the kids streaming into the building, thinking they look just like the kids who stream into my high school in Minnesota. Except there are more cowboy boots here. "Does this e-mail say anything in particular I should know about?"

"Only that I applied for early admission at the University of Oklahoma," Max says. "And that all we have to do now is sit around and wait for them to tell me if I got in or not."

The snap of the American flag on the nearby pole sounds like applause. "For real?"

"You bet it's for real."

I take a deep breath, telling myself that no matter what happens with Max, it's not about whether he ends up close to me. We both agreed caring about each other doesn't take being in the same place or being on the same chase team.

Though, make no mistake: getting both would be a giant solid.

"What about Vaughn Commodities Management? Won't your dad be upset if you're suddenly back in Oklahoma?"

"Probably."

"But you're just going to do it anyway?"

"Hell, yes."

There's not a single part of me that's surprised by his answer. "In that case, I want your college application to be the thing that makes it out of the twister."

"Except that wasn't an option."

"I might be playing a different version of the vortex game these days."

Max laughs. "Well, whatever the rules, I just wanted to tell you to have an awesome first day."

"Thanks," I say, meaning it.

"I'll talk to you tonight, okay?" Max asks.

"Okay," I say, "talk to you then." We end our call, and I walk the last few steps to the doors.

Right before I duck into the building, I take one last look at the sky. It's a brilliant blue, with long, hazy wisps of cloud floating here and there.

There's not a twister for miles.

ACKNOWLEDGMENTS

In 2004, when I booked my ticket on a weeklong tornado chase (the "tourist" kind), I never could have imagined that experience would inspire an entire manuscript. But it did, and I'm grateful to the many people who helped me take that seed of inspiration and grow it into this book.

My editor, Stacey Barney, deserves a cape and sparkly tights for the superhero-like way she always makes anything I write halfway palatable. And for telling me things like, no, you can't raise the stakes by introducing a vampire halfway through the story. Thank you for getting Jane through the storm.

And, as ever, thank you to my agent, Susanna Einstein, for her expert guidance and insight. *Pthith!!!caweib!!* ← Some days, I swear this is what I call her saying, and she always makes sense of it and steers me right. She deserves a pair of those sparkly tights too.

Thanks to the many writers who read and supported both Jane and me from chapter one. Susanna Nichols, Kelly O'Connor McNees, Ellen Baker, and Rhonda Stapleton—I'm looking at you. Thanks, too, to Neil Shurley for reaching out and supporting me through the magic of the Interwebs, and to Margaret Yang for taking my "character motivation" calls.

Daily I'm blessed by my friends in the College of LSA at the University of Michigan, as well as the women of Ypsi Studio, especially Julia Collins. I'm also surrounded by wonderful family who accommodate my crazy schedule and, at times, my even crazier attitude. Thanks for always asking how things are going and then handing me a glass of wine when all I can do is roll my eyes.

I'm supremely grateful to my steadfast cheering section of John Tebeau and Colleen Newvine. Pom-poms. You guys. Every time.

And finally, this book—as well as all of my others—wouldn't be possible without the herculean support and love of my husband, Rob. Who else will make sure my office is clean, the chocolate is stocked, and that I've got everything I need to finish my novels? Also, you don't hold your nose on day three of a showerless writing marathon, and you really probably should. Thanks for being the definition of awesome. You get me over the rainbow and back again—every time.